Happy
Rock

Also by Matthew Simmons

A Jello Horse

The Moon Tonight Feels My Revenge

HAPPY RCK

Matthew Simmons

DARK COAST PRESS
SEATTLE, WA

Dark Coast Press Company
3645 Greenwood Ave North
Seattle, Washington 98103
www.darkcoastpress.com
info@darkcoastpress.com

1 3 5 7 9 8 6 4 2
ISBN-13: 978-0-9850355-3-2

"We Never Ever Went to the Moon" first appeared in
The Nervous Breakdown,
"Father" first appeared in *Keyhole Magazine*, "Contents" first appeared in
TRNSFR, "Glory" first appeared in *Spork*, "Saxophone Lung Explodes" first
appeared in *The Sycamore Review*,
"College" first appeared in *Spork*, "Happy Rock" first appeared in *The
Fanzine*, "Anymore" first appeared in *Word Riot*, and "Daredevils" first
appeared in *Smalldoggies Magazine*

Cover design by Matthew Revert
Interior design by Corinne Manning
Distributed by Ingram Publisher Services
Printed in the United States of America

FOR DOC

The stars were packed so close that night
They seemed to press and stare
And gather in like hurdles bright
The liberties of air.

—Gerard Manley Hopkins

Go, Braves!

—Anonymous Gladstone High School football fan

contents

we never ever went to the moon

I will tell you this story, but only if you promise never to tell anyone else. I'm certain of much of it, and where I am not certain, I am comfortable making things up. Take that as a warning, I suppose. But the likelihood of inaccuracies is only one of the reasons why I ask for your confidence. The other reason will become plain as you listen. Altogether plain.

The two of them are sitting out under the stars, on the grass, and very close together. The moon is above, and broad. He, Matthew, is 16, as is she. Sarah is her name. They are friends—merely friends. They have kissed once, these two, after watching a movie together at dusk on a summer's night.

He was leaning toward her from his mother's living room chair, and had spent the last hour rubbing Sarah's shoulders with the tips of his fingers and his thumbs. She was in front of him, on the carpet, her back offered, with her right arm on his right knee, her right hand grazing his calf, and it felt to him like he was standing naked in a field and a tall blade of grass was swaying in a wind and brushing against him. He was ticklish then. She was as well. (Still is, if you wondered.) The hairs on his neck stiffened ever so slightly if her hand trailed too high up. He was 15 then, and felt the blood hurry to his lap. His thumbs padded up from her shoulders and into the twin trails of hair on the back of her neck. Her hair was short, and barely past her ears. Her neck was pale—a mole a dead center target. When the credits drifted up the screen, Matthew flipped the television off with the remote that was lying on the armrest, and Sarah turned up toward him. She was, quite suddenly, taken by a strange impulse. They smiled. There was a ceiling fan, and it whirred and spun above them, slowly stirring up the air. She rose up like a helium balloon, he bent down like coin knocked from a table. In other words, she too slowly, he too quickly. After a moment's anticipation, they kissed. There was a hint of moisture in the fumbling of soft lips. It lasted a minute or more, an hour or less, and ended. It passed. Things like that will pass. Impulses pass.

My life is marked by passing impulses, weird highway signs on a flat, Midwestern highway, advertising Mystery Spots, and encouraging a devotion to Jesus. And the rest is flat and empty. Not unpleasant. Just so.

In their late 30s, they will meet up again when she comes home to see about her family. They will talk a little about that kiss then. And they will talk about the other strange thing that happened when the two of them were together.

I'll tell about that next.

His parents moved them to Michigan and purchased a three-bedroom, three-bathroom ranch house on a bluff overlooking Bay de Noc. On the bluff is an 18-hole golf course. His family's only neighbor is the tee of the second hole. Everywhere else is jack pines, and sand, and bracken ferns. Matthew and Sarah are sitting on the fairway, perhaps two shots into the par four: one straight, long shot to hit the green, and then a putt for the hole. The green slopes east to west, but is smooth. They have used the rakes in the traps to write dirty words in the sand. He says: "Let's us scuttle across the sand trap like the little crabs at the beach!"

She asks him what the hell he is talking about. He shrugs.

Sarah lives on a small lake northeast of the bluff in an area without the ambient light of street lamps or neighbors. The road and her driveway are gravel. Her family owns dogs, two big shepherds, who bark when anyone pulls into the driveway, who hope very much to intimidate anyone who approaches, but who are, frankly, great cowardly pups without the wherewithal to protect the house in a real emergency. They sleep next to her, snoring and whimpering, and cower in closets when anyone in the house yells at anyone else.

Because it is dark there, the kind of dark that insists one use a flashlight from sundown to sunup, and because her father is the local high school science teacher—her high school science teacher, Matthew's high school science teacher—she knows her constellations, and has known them since her father taught them to her at 11 years of age, out on the dock behind the house. She is showing them to Matthew this night. She points to Draco, its tail twisted around the Little Dipper, and then cut off by the trees surrounding the fairway. She looks east and points to Pegasus. "Which would be the wings and which would be the legs?" he asks. The hours pass and Pegasus gallops behind them, and they look north to the top of Ursa Major. Hercules follows to the west. Sarah is the first to see the weird light in the sky.

"Is it a planet?" Matthew asks.

"I don't think so," Sarah says.

"Planets are like that, aren't they? Brighter and bigger?" There is something in the sky and it is getting bigger. It is a small, round spot, bright and also blue.

"Mhm. But, that's not one, I don't think. It's getting bigger."

"Shooting star?"

"Airplane?"

"Coming at us? Want another drink?" Matthew asks. They are drinking white wine from a jelly jar. Matthew sneaks a bit from the bottles his father has on hand. Little by little, he fills the jar. An inch here and an inch there, and his dad's never the wiser. He hides the jar behind books on a bookshelf in his room. It sits behind his William Burroughs novels. Sarah reaches over and grabs the jar. Their hands touch, but it is not a remarkable experience. They hold hands sometimes. They have hugged. They are familiar with what it's like when there is an impact of their skins. It is mostly comfortable. And a pity, as it always is when touching becomes familiar and loses its charge. The charge from the kiss is long, long gone. As I said, these things pass at that age. Even in a year.

Especially in a year.

The light, at the nape of the neck of Perseus, gets bigger and bigger. It happens very quickly. They watch, bemused, and it breaks apart, reveals itself to be a field of smaller lights. The smaller lights grow, break apart, and they, too, are made up of smaller lights.

Oh, and they are also getting high. I nearly forgot about that. Matthew has forgotten to bring his bowl home from his locker at school, so they are using a soda can. They have pushed two little dents into the empty can, and made an indent for the pot on top. He punched holes into it with the awl on his pocketknife. On the bottom, they have made a carb. They can suck the smoke in through the regular opening on top of the can, the hole through which one drinks. It is inefficient, but it does the job. It is in Matthew's hand, a red ember is dying in the recess.

The pot is weak. Mostly, it is shake from the bottom of the bag. Matthew plans to steal a twenty from his father's wallet the next day, and then he will ride his bike into Gladstone to see his friend, who is a dealer. Sarah never buys weed, and does not trust her folks to find it when they search through her room, a practice they started when one of them discovered a condom in her pocket.

Sadly, it was not a condom that she was carrying as a real-life precautionary measure, but one that she absently grabbed from the glove compartment of her older brother's car. All that fuss over a condom with no assigned penis to wear it. All that fuss.

"Is it a meteor shower?"

She doesn't answer. The small lights fill the sky, and then they fall to earth and pepper the fairway. They, Sarah and Matthew, don't run. Because, really, why would they? They watch as around them a phosphorescent snow falls. When the lights hit the grass, they sizzle and disappear into the dewy ground. Larger pieces melt more slowly. They bounce off of Sarah and Matthew's shoes. And then there is a large one. Matthew will—talking about it later—say, "Darn thing made a beeline for my yapper." He gulps it down. When it drops into his stomach, whatever it is begins to boil. His muscles twitch and seize, and he clamps his eyes down tight as waves pulse out from the lump in his stomach.

Sarah sees a large piece on the ground, crackling and shedding layers. She kneels down, puts her hands out, feels no heat, and she feels no cold. She scoops it up, the light illuminating her face. If Matthew's eyes weren't closed, he'd see her in the pale blue light incandescing in her hands. The shard crackles again, tickles her palms, splits in two and burrows down through her hands and into her arms. She feels her arms stiffen and fill, her elbows straighten, and her shoulders shrug, like an involuntary shudder in the cold winter of Upper Michigan. But this is something else: this is something growing in her forearms.

And here is where it gets weird. The thing that fell from the sky that he then swallowed? It rattles around and around in his belly, and it cuts the cords of gravity. You probably didn't know this, but gravity works because we are all born with an invisible cord in our bellies, and those cords are what hold us down. The cord runs all the way to the center of the Earth, where they all attach to each other in a huge knot. We, all of us, hold each other to the Earth.

That's his theory, anyway. That's how he explains the whole thing to her. His cord is cut, and he finds that he can fly, if he puts his mind to it.

He flies. And something has happened to her, too. The burrowing, bright objects from the sky that have settled in her arms can project a material out of the center of her palms, where little stigmatic holes open and close. It grows out, a sort of a transparent bronzy substance. She can will it to spin out of her, like a web, and use it to make long ropes, or she can cover herself in a shell that is impossible to crack. It is hard or soft depending on what she wants. And she can make the stuff disappear whenever she wants, too. It smells vaguely organic, mossy. The scent mingles well with the rosewater perfume she wears. She smells a little like the woods for the rest of her life. It is, she feels lucky, not at all an unpleasant odor. People tell her that she smells outdoorsy, and that they think of her sometimes when they go hiking.

They call themselves Cocoon Lass and the Astounding Traveler. And they never tell a soul. Not one. They promise to keep it a secret forever from everyone. And they never break that promise.

Or they expect to never break that promise. This conversation, I suppose, is a little bit of all-bets-are-off.

In high school, she gets in the middle of fights, a thin

impenetrable layer of brown beneath her clothes. She confronts bullies who pick on the younger, smaller, meeker students. Because of that, almost everybody likes her. She is a fearless crusader for justice.

Or something like that.

His grades fall and never recover. He spends his time looking out the window and never really finds a girlfriend. He sleeps at his school desk because he stays up all night. Teachers chastise him, but eventually just ignore him. He is beyond their help.

Things are otherwise pretty normal for them. She follows in her father's footsteps and becomes a teacher. She is not afraid of anything, so she decides she will become a teacher in inner city Chicago. She will write to Matthew now and then, and tell him how things are going. If she feels even a little afraid, she knows that she can cover herself up in her unbreakable, golden cocoons. Other teachers admire her for never backing down from problem students. Under her shirt, she keeps a solid brown shell. And sometimes, she makes a little bit of it in her hand, and rubs it with her thumb without really thinking about it. It will feel like a little pebble, a pebble smoothed in a lake that she would pick up and take around with her in her pocket. She grows little pebbles and keeps them in her hand.

He doesn't leave home. He stays in Gladstone, and gets a job at a pet casket factory. They make pet caskets out of hard, beige, stippled sheets of plastic. The sheets are heated, and pressed in forms. When a sheet is formed into a piece of the casket—say, the lid—the machine makes a thunk. The caskets are leak-proof and worm-proof, and can have a comfortable lining added to them at a reasonable cost.

She asks him about the job.

He says he works with guys who refer to magazines as "books," and smoke on the job. Matthew smells of melting chemicals and his coworkers' cigarettes.

She says he could, if he wanted, not live in Gladstone anymore. He could move some place, like Chicago. Or Milwaukee. He could come and stay with her for a little while, get situated, have a better job, read her books and sleep on her couch for a while. He wouldn't be a burden.

He doesn't care. Every night, he drinks beer and soars off into the sky. He has never saved anyone, and has never been spotted. He has never even helped a neighbor get a cat out of a tree. He drinks his beer in cans: Hamms, and Schaeffer, and Pabst Blue Ribbon. He drinks his beer and flies off into the sky. And he goes wherever he wants, too.

She reminds him that if he wanted, he could probably save people. He could, conceivably, be astounding.

He likes to fly late at night when there is no chance he will be spotted. He says wants to stay where he is, where there aren't many buildings, or people who stay up all night and look out their windows. He tells her that's what the city is to him: a place where he would inevitably be spotted. And then he might be asked to save someone. He might have to start wearing a mask. "And you know where that would lead, Sarah. A cape. It would inevitably lead to a cape. No one wants that."

One night, soon after they develop their powers, they decide they will find out just how high up he can go. She lashes a little bit of her cocoon stuff to his ankle, and he ascends. "Pull the tether if you feel faint. I'll see you falling and make a big cushion for you if you pass out," she says.

He goes up so far that she can't see him. Eventually, she can't keep making her cocoon tether, and, after a sudden pull, it goes slack. The tether tumbles from the sky, and makes a pile next to her. She wishes it away, and it fades away. It takes him hours to come back.

Matthew tells her he went all the way to the moon.

She has always liked the moon, and always wondered about it. She makes a little crescent moon in her hand when he says that, does it without thinking. It just comes out. When she notices, she doesn't wish it away. She leaves it there.

In Chicago, she dates. Sometimes, she sees a man she met at a rock 'n' roll show. When they met, they got into a discussion about how all indie rock bands had girl bass players named Kim. She told him she wished she were named Kim, because then she could be the bass player for a band. They made out later, drank red wine on her couch, and he told her he really admired her for being a teacher.

When she breaks up with that guy for the last time—there will be a number of breakups with that guy, each more messy and unpleasant than the last—she will feel, deep down inside, as if she is doing it because she does not think she is worthy of his admiration, because why should Cocoon Lass be afraid of anything?

But, really, maybe they just aren't right for each other. It will take a while for this to occur to her.

Matthew's room is mostly empty, except for a mini fridge, a silver floor lamp with a round glass shade for the bulb, and a Silver Surfer poster. He also has a Silver Surfer t-shirt that he wears too much. It has holes worn into it and a stretched-out neck. He still likes to get high and listen to music. He takes music with him whenever he flies. His paychecks from the pet casket factory pay for rent, beer, cassette tapes, batteries, and weed.

She writes him letters and asks about the moon. He tells her all about it. She asks about the silence, and the absence of oxygen, and the dead gray dust and rock. He tells her it's not like that at all, and that the moon has oceans, just like Earth, and oxygen, just like Earth, and even plants, just like Earth. Only, yes, the surface is grayer in places. It is like a paler Earth, he says. She writes again and tells him he is full of shit, because she has seen footage of the moon landing, and knows precisely what the moon is like. He tells her he is the one who has been there, not her. He is, in fact, the only person who has ever been there, he says. She's unsure what to say in her next letter, so his claim goes unanswered. She can't write back. He writes again.

"We didn't really go to the moon," he writes. "The moon landing was a hoax. We've never been there. Well, I have, but we (mankind) haven't (hasn't)."

She sends him another letter and it is a single page, and it looks like this:

> Matthew,
> ?

She doesn't even sign it.

Many letters follow. He sends her evidence of the hoaxed Moon landing. He sends citations for websites. Photocopies of photographs and pages from what look to be self-published magazines and books.

"Why," he asks her, "are there no stars in the pictures even though they are in space?"

"Why," he asks her, "does the American flag that they plant on the Moon appear to be swaying in the breeze when there would be no breeze on the Moon?"

"Why," he asks her, "do all the photos seem to have the same group of hills behind them when the astronauts supposedly went from place to place to explore the surface of the moon?"

"Why," he asks her, "is there no blast crater from the landing?"

"Why," he asks her, "didn't all the astronauts die from all the radiation they were exposed to when they passed the Van Allen Belt in space?"

Sarah finds answers to every one of these questions, and she writes back. He finds more evidence of the Moon landing hoax, and he sends it. And, again, she finds answers to all his questions; she refutes all his evidence. Finally, he writes this:

"Why do you continue to believe all the things you read instead of believing the testimony of someone who has actually been there to the moon? You've spoken to me. Spoken to Neal Armstrong? Met Neal Armstrong? Sure Neal Armstrong is an actual person? Certain? Absolutely stone certain?"

And, really, she's not sure how to answer that, so she doesn't. So with that she goes on with her life for a time, as if maybe we—humanity in general, and NASA specifically—didn't really go to the moon.

She comes home to see about her folks. I mentioned that this would happen. Her father is getting older, and her mother is starting to have trouble with him. He forgets things sometimes, for example to wear his shoes outside. He starts leaving his keys in the refrigerator. So she comes home.

Her mother asks her about Matthew. "Is he really still here?" she says.

"Yeah," she says. "I'm going to go see him tomorrow, maybe."

"You should," her mother says. "Talk some sense into him."

"Oh," Sarah says, "that's not very likely."

Sarah spends time with her father, sitting on the dock behind their house, and looking out at the water. He sits quietly for the most part, though at one point he starts to laugh. He just starts to laugh, and Sarah looks over at him to see what is funny. "What's funny, Dad," she says.

"Was I laughing," he says, laughing. "I didn't notice."

Sarah goes to see Matthew a few days later. She insists that she needs proof. She wants him to prove that we never, ever went to the moon.

He agrees to take her with him to the moon, and in fact has a well thought out plan of action. He tells her to make a bubble for herself, a cocoon in which to ride. Small so he can carry it, but big enough for her to be comfortable. Big enough for a sleeping bag so she won't be cold in space. He says she will need an oxygen tank for the trip through space to the moon, and lots of warm clothes; he has a nice sleeping bag, too, one he can loan her. He has all these things in his garage, waiting.

It is very early in the morning when he leaves his apartment to pick her up. He is very quiet when he turns the bolt on his door. He gathers the things he has prepared from his garage, putting them in a large canvas knapsack. He lowers the garage door to the concrete apron very gently. He is as quiet as he can when he steps into the alley behind his apartment, and, when he is sure he is alone, lifts himself into the sky. The distant moon, round and mottled with gray-blue spots, is still out.

He arrives in back of her family's house, and she is sitting behind a sliding glass door, reading on the couch. No dogs are there to bark anymore. They have long since passed away.

He doesn't need to knock. She slips out through the door, and pulls on a heavy jacket. There's a nice open area of lawn where she builds her traveling cocoon. It has a cord on the end that wraps around his ankle. He takes off, and her cocoon follows him up a moment later. He flies fast, and she is right behind him.

During the flight, they keep in contact by walkie-talkie, except when they are in space and there is no air to fill his lungs. He calls her when they arrive on the moon. "The light has changed," she says.

"Welcome to the Sea of Storms," he tells her. "Ever wonder why they call it that? Now you know. Rain!"

As they fly, a pattering plays against the bubble. It sounds like nervous fingers tapping. She calls him.

"Will we go down to the surface?" she asks.

"Soon," he says. "Very, very soon."

She prods and she prods, and eventually he finds the spot and takes her to the surface. She makes the bubble disappear, and steps down. Her feet sink a bit into the gray sand of the moon. She gazes out over an ocean.

"The Sea of Serenity," he tells her.

The waves attack, fall back, attack, fall back. She walks to a clump of brown grass, and she stops.

"Why don't I bounce? Why don't I feel any different? Lighter?" she asks.

"Oh, gravity. Another scientific theory. That's all it is, you know. Just a theory."

Sarah stares and Matthew looks away. She kneels down, and runs her fingers through the sand. She sifts out a rock, a shell, then a cigarette butt. She looks back at Matthew who sees the cigarette butt in her hand and looks away.

"That's mine," Matthew says. "I come here a lot."

"Where are we?" she asks.

The waves attack the shore. The waves fall back. The palm trees behind them rustle.

"The moon," he says.

"Matthew, where are we?"

The waves attack the shore.

"Somewhere. Australia, I guess."

"We're in Australia?" she asks. Matthew nods and scratches his left knee. "What is this? Why is the sand so gray?"

"Oh, I ... sort of," he says, "made it."

"You made this?"

"It's kind of a set."

"It's a set?"

"I made a ... set. Sets."

"Sets?"

"A few." The waves attack the shore. Sarah raises a hand to her forehead to cover her eyes from the sun. She looks out over the water.

"A few?"

"I thought you might like to see the moon."

"Can you?"

"No. Too high, Can't breathe. Too cold. No moon. No moon for me!" he says, and he laughs nervously.

Somewhere out on the water, a loud, deep horn sounds, one short burp, one long. The noise stumbles on to shore.

"You're weird."

"Kind of. I probably should have thought this through better."

The waves attack the shore. In the distance, a cruise ship wanders by, the passengers on board are drunk and playing shuffle board.

"Chicago has some very quiet neighborhoods," she says. "It really does."

Would you be let down if you found out nothing will happen here? Would it disappoint you to know that Sarah and Matthew will not, in this moment, find comfort in each other? Would not fall into one another?

If you found out that something did happen here, would this story, with its all-too-familiar happy ending, strain credibility? Would it be overcome by sentimentality? Because this is not a sentimental story. Not in the least. This is just the truth. Or mostly the truth, and some embellishments.

We could have gone either way, the two of us. Any of us. And you no doubt see my dilemma. You see the danger in this moment.

I will say this: I still live in Chicago, although I retired from teaching a long time ago.   Under my shirt, I still have an amber carapace, and I fear almost nothing because of it. I am old and I leave my keys in the refrigerator. I look out the window at the moon and imagine that we've never been there. Not a single, damned one of us.

Instead of the ending, though, let's go back to months before the scene at the beach.

There's a day when he is flying around the continent of Australia with a book of moon landing photos in his hand. He knows he doesn't have to be exactly right because he has told her the moon is just like the Earth, but he wants a place that is remote, and he wants something somewhat like the pictures in the book. He circles and he circles until he finds the right beach.

And that night he goes home and writes her a letter. His father has died. His mother has died.

So he has plenty of time. There isn't anything else for him to think about. He wonders if maybe he should start exercising and eating better and maybe not drink so much.

He finds gray sand and carries it to the beach. He covers a large section of the beach with it, bucket by bucket. It takes a long time, weeks. In slow runs, he strafes the beach, pouring sand in fuzzy edged trails.

the residents

Dusk and the Sparrow boy sits at his window and watches the vans bring the residents home. In the morning, the vans take the residents away and he watches that, too.

And he watches when vans pull up to the back, and a gurney is wheeled out the service entrance of the building. That can happen at any time: in the morning, at dusk, in the middle of the day, in the middle of the night. Merely nine years old, the Sparrow boy knows that anyone can go at any time.

The residents gamble away each day, eight at a time climbing into a van with the name of this or that casino painted on the side. Eight climb in, eight drive off, eight come back, eight more climb in. The Sparrow boy watches the residents cycle through the days, going out to gamble away their money, on their way back to enter the glass and stucco building they call home: The Bishop Lee Home for Seniors.

Right now, there is an older boy sitting in his father's van at the building's service entrance. He is listening, once again, to a tape he made for a girl. She had given it back before she left for college. Last year. Next to him is another, with light brown skin and the goatee, a partner, making a face at the older boy, and his eyes say this again. The older boy's face returns no apology. It returns nothing.

The Sparrow boy is slight and freckled and his father often calls him Tank in mocking contradiction to his frame. He had an infection in his legs, and had to remain at home in bed throughout the summer. That's when he started watching the residents. His father carried him from room to room. His brother put him in a wagon and took him for walks, up and down the block. Sometimes, they would leave him under a tree in the yard to read. He walks fine now, but is still spending the last days of summer in his room or in his yard.

The older boy and his partner enter the service entrance at the resident's home, and follow one of the caretakers to a room on the third floor. The caretaker asks after the older boy's father, and wonders when the older boy expects to leave for college. Will he be coming back to take over his father's business? The answers are tersely given, but the caretaker takes no offense. He figures it is just the way of those in the boy's profession.

The Sparrow boy sits under the tree.

The residents cycle in and out.

With the caretaker watching at the door, the two of them count to three and lift the resident out of his bed and onto the gurney. They use his bed sheet. Once, they had to pick up a newborn. The case they used looked like a briefcase. It disturbed a nurse, until they opened it up and showed her that the inside was soft. The comfortable lining was only comforting to the nurse, not the newborn. The resident is wheeled out to the van. He will soon be in the basement of a funeral home, where he will be drained, and the older boy will slowly massage fluid into the body, one limb at a time.

The Sparrow boy is standing by the van when the older boy and his partner come out. The older boy looks at the Sparrow boy, but the Sparrow boy stares at the sheet on the gurney. And stares. The legs collapse as the gurney is shoved into the van. The partner steps away for a cigarette, and he calls someone on a cell phone. He speaks to the person on the other end, lovingly.

The older boy starts the van, and the tape begins to play. He opens the passenger door, and the Sparrow boy climbs in at the older boy's prompting. The older boy pulls the sheet away, and allows the Sparrow boy a few minutes to ask his questions directly to the prone, silent resident. The Sparrow boy whispers.

The residents are gathering for dinner.

father

We're living in sin in the Keweenaw Peninsula with a big-ass Mastiff we call Father. And this is it, miles from anyone, no one bothers us anymore. Father must weigh upwards of 200 pounds, and has a motley face, with a huge frown and tiny black eyes.

I call, "Father, c'mon back, boy," and he runs through the snow, bounding through the jack pines and if you didn't know him like I know him, it would most certainly scare something like the fear of Hell into you. He lets out grunts as he approaches; huffing as he leaps up, then hits the snow, breaks through, and sinks down. Leaps up again, arcs above the deep, settled white snow on the ground, breaks through, and sinks down again. Snow's deep this year.

None of the family knows where we've gotten to. That's all right with us. And I have a mind to, sometime soon, put a baby in her just to see what comes out. Just now, though, we let it fall to the ground, though we know that to be a sin. We're not ready, and God knows. So, she says, "Just on the belly," and I let go on her belly.

On Father's birthday, we sit him at the dinner table, and put a red, white, orange, and blue party hat on him. He's good about it and doesn't make a fuss. Father'd snap your wrist when you went at him with a colorful cardboard cone about to affix to the top of his head with a rubber band around his chin, if he was so inclined. But, when it comes to us, Father has no such inclination. He desires only our gracious attention, and whatever happens to be on the dinner plates at the table. And that's just what Father gets.

She says: "Remorse is for other people. Not for us. Missing everyone and wishing they were here is for other people. Not for us." We have all we need. We heat our home with a wood stove, and use heavy blankets on our bed. The food here should hold out just long enough. We have each other. I have her and she has me.

She is quiet and gentle, and the light cast by her soul bursts the seams of the walls of this cabin. I swear it does.

And she says, "You anchor me to the ground. I'd have floated away long ago without you."

When He comes back someday, we'll be ready for him. He will recognize us as husband and wife, and we won't be punished for anything we've done in the past. We're following Him up. We're redeemed by the Blood of the Lamb.

Father sleeps at the foot of our bed, and he snores an awful lot like my own father used to. My mother eventually kicked my father to the couch, all the noise he made. Father, the dog, can stay as long as he likes; we sleep soundly.

When Father hears a noise outside, he will lift up his head, and give a low bark that flaps his cheeks out. Mastiffs were bred to guard the home. Father spends a lot of his day sitting on our front porch, body in a ready-pose, but relaxing, too.

Father's kind used to circle the ancient cities of Babylon in packs, warding off attackers.

When the Redeemer comes to the door, Father will lower his head in a respectful bow. We will hold up our son or daughter to the Lamb of God and He will bless him or her, and baptize the child in the sink or with water from a bottle.

Our old college friends live in Chicago, Kansas City or Portland, Oregon. They share their homes with (in order of frequency) Chocolate Labs, Vizlas, rescued Greyhounds, and a Burmese Mountain dog. They get dressed up in fleece and running shoes and bring them to nearby off-leash parks. We used to write to them, and many would respond to ask if we were well. They were married in churches and civil ceremonies. They have their matrimonial bonds recognized by state and federal governments. That strikes us as all wrong. But, then, who are we to judge?

She once got a blinding headache, where purple dots danced and crowded in her eyes. She ground her teeth so loud, she woke Father from a nap. She said it was lightning in her brain.

I had her lie down, and put on a wet cloth. I covered her face with my hands and asked Our Lord for help, and by and by, the pain dissolved. We thanked Him for his mercy, and the headache never came back.

o

Father is quick to forgive when we yell at him or at each other in his presence. He sidles over to us, and stares up. A little white in his eye shows, just at the edge, like a sliver of the waning moon.

She says, "Panic is a tingle in the jaw that makes your mouth water. That's how it gets to your belly—when you swallow your saliva, the panic follows it down. Panic is a little feeling that wanders by, and you invite it in because you don't want to ignore it like you should. Panic is the loudest voice in the room, even though it comes from the tiniest person." She says, "Blue was the color of 50 milligrams of Zoloft. Yellow was the color of 100. When they moved me from blue and asked me to start taking yellow, I knew I was getting worse instead of better. And I knew that meant it was time to find something else." She's doing fine, now, without her little yellow pills.

She made me understand the way I felt sometimes. She brought me to a better understanding of God's love, and showed me how He, ever so gently, severed you from your pain. She showed me by learning how to see on her own. She showed me by her actions, how she lived her life.

The three of us met in college. Father was locked in a crate 20 hours a day in the basement of the home of a certain Professor Nagle, a teacher of comparative religion. It sickened us to think of him there. That's why we took him with us when we left.

We were asked over for dinner one night, and met Father. This Professor Nagle called him crate-trained. He told us the crate was in Father's nature; he told us every dog needs a den. But that was surely not comfort we heard in Father's howls. When we were asked to take care of Professor Nagle's place, we let Father free of his cage. He wandered the house after us, and slept between us on the professor's huge bed, dreaming and kicking us with his legs.

When Professor Nagle returned, and we told him what we'd done, he said he was disappointed. He would ask us again, someday, to watch his home, but only if we kept Father crated. House rules, he said.

Better for him to spend most of his time in his crate, he insisted. Get used to it eventually, he was sure.

We took Father and beat it out of that town. We left our student loans behind us and didn't look back. We went north, here to the Keweenaw. We sold the professor's car to pay the rent on our new home. (People ask fewer questions than you figure they will.) Father spent the first three days outside running, and his back and legs got visibly stronger with each passing week. All that pent up energy was finally released. Father was a marvel to watch: his long, bouncing strides pushing him up and forward; his mouth wide and tongue lolling.

Right from the beginning, her mother said she didn't want to hear any of our born again crap from us. I told her, frankly, we could care less if she was or not. Conversations on the phone with her father ended with her holding the phone away from her, loud squawks coming from the earpiece. She'd smile and roll her eyes, and wait for the volume to get lower. She'd thank Daddy, and laugh and eventually just hang up.

It's not like either of us hear Him speak to us directly, or through the voices of angels, or in messages written in the sky, or see Him manifested in yellow crystals in the snow after Father marks his territory, but I do feel Him. We feel Him. We feel Him in the frozen air we inhale, taking Father for a walk.

She says she recognizes His art in the snow that covers the

branches of the pines. I say I feel Him in her fingers, when they rest on my shoulder at night.

I see Him in the tumble of red hair on the pillow beside me. I hear Him in the morning whimper she makes; the one that makes me think she would sleep forever if she could.

I see Him in the black spatter of polka dots on the pink edge of Father's nose.

We have things in common. Things from the past. We have liquor bottles, and pot pipes, and pills, and being brought to strangers to talk about what was bothering us. We both had little patterned razor-blade cuts hidden on our thighs. We both met Jesus, and one day gave ourselves to Him. And with His help, we started to turn our backs on everything that had damaged us.

My father was in his 60's when I was born—an old man for what little of my life he saw. He passed when I was five. He was a jowly man, and the wide, sinking cheeks, the rubber of his face are the only things about him I remember.

He looks like my father, I said to her when we saw the dog the first time, and the name stuck. Dad was in Korea. I have his old herringbone jacket, green and beaten up, with an Indian-head patch of the 2nd Infantry Division. Mother said he was a Methodist from Yakima, Washington. He took care of her, and she left him anyway, even though he was in poor health, and wouldn't have needed to commit to him very long before he was gone.

When we met in college, we both had broken homes, and Jesus. But we didn't so much know Him back then—not like now—as we thought there was a lot about Him to like. What good was that? What good were our Sundays in the school chapel? Or the

Campus Crusade for Christ? Our friends in fellowship? What good was any of it when it was only half way? What good was any of it when it was simply a public face we were wearing? When it was just a slogan in a t-shirt? A fashion we were into? We met a man who helped us beyond all that. And then, we saw through his way, as well. And we left, and found our way here.

He set out a rug in the Pentacrest in the middle of campus, and knelt down in prayer. Now she points out: "They love to pray standing in the synagogues and on the corners of the streets . . . " We just talked to him. He explained things—the things we'd never really understood in what we'd read. He made things clearer. He walked with us in tow, chastising those around him. Young girls for their skirts, young boys for the lust they directed at young girls. He was like what we imagine John the Precursor was like—that burning in his eyes. And he was so young, his face was still marked by acne. We followed him, for a while. But, we saw pride in him, eventually, and we left him for our own path. We saw the way he flaunted his faith—the way he looked for his reward in the devotion of others to him. We knew when to stop. We knew when the crowd around him was getting too big. He called himself Joshua.

Imagine it like this: our breath will be visible in the slightest whisper, every word made opaque. The house will shake, and we'll run to the window, and He'll ride down on a cloud. He'll smile as He steps through our door. He'll accept us as we accept Him. And Father will be on his very best behavior.

We cut our hair and we bought plainer clothes and we moved into a house with Joshua. He talked endlessly, and talked always about the End of Days. And we listened. And we missed what we should have caught—most of all, the certainty in Joshua's voice. The certainty that he walked with the Son of Man. He had no trouble with it, with faith. His vision was clear, he thought. He asked us to honor our parents, but reject their way. So, we did. He asked us to drop out of school, rejecting that way, too. So, we did. But his certainty became an insult to the One he claimed to serve.

We asked too many questions. We quoted too many things back to him—his words, sometimes, or the words of the prophets. Once or twice, she left Joshua speechless with a carefully chosen word or two. To him, we had gone wicked. He pointed to the door, but we were mostly out of it already.

By Providence, we had met Professor Nagle on the street and he had asked if we could look after Father for him.

Father was there, waiting. His crate had been moved under the stairs, in the darkest part of the professor's basement. We heard him whine as we descended the steps.

She pulled the chain on a bare, hanging light bulb, and we walked along the concrete to him. He pushed his paws out of the bars, reaching for us. She got down, first. She leaned in as close as she could, and Father's tongue stuck out and wetted her face. He pushed as much of his body as he could into the gate, nose and paws and teeth trying to get out the small square openings. We laughed and pushed back at him, trying to unlock the gate latch. We couldn't let Father out soon enough.

On the day we left the world behind us, we first brought Father out to a dog park. He'd never been to one. We drove down in the car Professor Nagle had left for us to use. Father took to the park, and found himself a pack to run with while we relaxed on a bench. We had taken a long walk around the park's big, looping dirt path, watched the dogs jump into the cold water of Lake Superior. It was fall. We watched him run through the field of mud with four others, all of whom deferred to him. He was giant among them—the hounds and the labs stayed at his flanks, a respectful step behind his long lope. They kicked up mud clumps behind them, and turned quick and precise like a bird flock, Father at the lead. They disappeared around the left and reappeared around the right side of a small hill. They swam in grass to their shoulders. They made a slalom of the dog owners playing fetch and tug-of-war with their pets. They pulled in and shed pack members, dogs sloughing off into the tall grass for a rest. Always Father at the lead. They started for an old woman sunning herself, and holding the leashes of two small dogs. We didn't notice until it was way too late, but Father was wilding. All that time, locked away, who could blame him? One of the old woman's leashes was ripped from her hand, pulled her forward. She grabbed for the fence to steady herself. Her mouth hung open, but she didn't make a sound. Father had snatched her Pomeranian up as he ran by. He snapped a little dog's neck, shaking his head in a blur. Father and the pack had moved on, the Pomeranian dropped in a puddle of muddy rainwater and blood. Its tiny body was limp, and its gold fur was dark and moist. The woman began to scream. As a crowd gathered, we called Father over, and ran with him to the professor's car. We didn't bother toweling the mud from Father's legs, or the blood and drool from his chin. We put him in the backseat and drove away, and left town that night. No one had time to stop us, but someone in the gathering crowd threw a rock at the car, denting the trunk. Father, contrite, watched them crowding around the woman, on her knees in the mud. Her other dog was jumping up on her, pushing her with his paws, asking to be held.

o

It's winter and the Peninsula is cut off from the rest of the U.P. right now. But we listen anyway. We listen and Father listens for any sounds in the trees. They'll show up, eventually. But maybe not before He does. That's what we count on—we count on him making us invisible to the outside world. To the Nagles. To the Joshuas. To the families. To the friends. What use are they?

He will wipe away our tears, as his spirit has done so many times before. His fingers will brush our cheeks.

He who sits in the heavens shall laugh.

contents

Contents of a bedroom nightstand drawer, January 6, 8 a.m., Gladstone, Michigan

Pill bottle, Sertraline, six left.

Pill bottle, Alprazolam, empty.

Pen, blue ink, three quarters full.

Pen, black ink, almost empty.

Notebook, nine and a half by six inches, 80 sheets (nine removed), college-ruled, three quarters full, mostly drawings, non sequiturs, three dated entries.

Box of condoms, four left, five empty wrappers stuck back in the box.

Small flashlight.

Double A (AA) batteries, two.

Contents of a wallet, March 7, 6 p.m., Escanaba, Michigan

$16.50, two $5, six $1, and another $1 bill torn in half, it's mate in a wallet in Milwaukee, Wisconsin.

Subway sub card, five punches.

Mastercard credit/debit card.

Wallet-sized school photo of a girl, inscribed "xoxo, laurie".

Public library card, significantly faded signature.

Spare house key.

Book of stamps, two left.

Business card, mental health counselor.

Contents of an envelope, April 6, 3 p.m., Gladstone, Michigan

$400 in cash.

One note, nine and a half by six inches, blue ink, mostly apologies, resigned tone.

Contents of a uterus, May 19, 5 p.m., Marquette, Michigan

Traces of old blood, amniotic fluid, and cervical mucus.

Strings of fetal tissue and muscle from the uterine wall.

Bits of placenta.

Contents of the interior pocket of a denim jacket, June 3, Noon, Gladstone, Michigan

Pack of spearmint chewing gum, two pieces left.

Cigarette lighter, green plastic, half-empty.

Plastic baggie, marijuana, $6 or so left, mostly shake, seeds, and a dry, crumbling bud.

Brass one-hitter.

Note from an ex-girlfriend, lined college-ruled notebook paper, blue ink, faded, insincere tone, mildly insulting assumptions, confusing meaning.

Plastic sunglasses, green plaid pattern, cat's eye shape.

Contents of the woods behind a house, June 3, 7 p.m, Gladstone, Michigan

Trees, mostly jack pines.

13 and one half squirrels. (Three young, counted as half.)

Fort made of flat, uneven plywood sheets.

Innumerable acorns.

A couple thousand square feet of moss.

38 birds. (More moments earlier.)

24 hidden pornographic magazines in an elementary school student's stash under a sheet in the fort, wrapped in a plastic bag.

427 cigarette butts.

Bullet casing for a .30 - .30 Winchester.

The skeletons of five cats, two buried under headstones.

Male, age 17, stoned, bleeding from the abdomen.

One rare Lady's slipper, purple flute, white petals.

Contents of a shot glass, June 8, 1 a.m., Escanaba, Michigan

Half a fluid ounce of Rye whiskey.

The impression of the bottom of a lip, cherry red lipstick, recently applied.

saxophone lung explodes

My dad is standing in front of a line of life-sized, clay copies of my dear, dead mother. They are in the garage, standing at something like parade rest, tipped back on their ankles, stiff bodies against the wall. I'm hidden outside the door, and he's choosing which one he is going to use next.

The family car has been parked on the lawn ever since he turned the garage into his private mother workshop.

My mom, she'll be back soon—until one of us manages to upset her. This means she will once again be walking around from room to room in our house, silent except for the thud of her heavy, flat-footed steps. And she'll sit with us at dinner, even though she won't eat. And she'll be in the kitchen, staring out the window when I get off work. She'll be sitting on the couch in the morning when we get up, and she'll leave a little clay dust on the dark fabric cushion when she rises—a little imprint on the hand rest, a little silhouette behind her head. My dead mother back among the living—though certainly not living herself. Not living at all. Just close enough—apparently—for Dad.

He has picked out a comfortable pair of sweatpants, a collared shirt, and a blue cardigan for her to wear. The sweater has an ivory cameo above the breast. All the mothers are propped up against the wall, and he's walking up and down the row, trying to choose.

I've never seen this part. I don't know how he does it. I don't know how he chooses, and I don't know how he animates these lumps of mud—stuffed beneath a layer of clay as they are with things, with objects that belonged to the living, real her—and makes them move around and act as a stand-in, because I've never wanted to see it. I've watched the mothers being built, but I've never seen them come to life.

Or come to whatever it is they come to. Not life, though. Certainly not life.

Sorry. I misspoke.

I'd made a promise to myself that I would try hard to no longer yell at Dad. So, instead, I had decided to yell at our lawyer. We were in his office for our annual visit, my dad and me, in two brown leather chairs; the lawyer was turned to the window, looking out through the slats of the open shades. "There has to be something you can do," I said. "What good was the living will if Dad can just breach it like this? She said do not resuscitate. Her instructions were very clear." Dad creaked against the leather of his chair.

"I don't know if you can really say that your," and our lawyer bit his nail and hesitated before he said, "mother has been resuscitated."

"She breathes. Or, does something like breathing. Her chest seems to expand and contract. Isn't that resuscitated? And she's here. She's out there. Look at her," I said, pointing out the window at our car. The model I was calling Saxophone Lung—there are four models, and I have named each by the stuff Dad uses to fill their torsos—was sitting in the back seat, still belted in and moving very little. Our Pekapoo, Glory, was in the front passenger seat, her nose stuck out the cracked window, and she was straining up to catch scents on the air. She was clamoring, her paws slipping against the glass, as she struggled to force her muzzle farther out. "Just look at that. Look at Glory even trying to ignore her. You have to tell him to stop."

"We go through this every year. I really don't think—" said our lawyer.

"Dad, come on," I said. "She wouldn't have wanted this." I stared at my father. He was wearing his old brown suit, and a deep burgundy tie. The suit he bought and wore to his retirement party a few years back. He always dressed up when I forced him to come with me to see the lawyer. He was stooped over in his chair and he was staring at his hands, which were draped between the knees of brown corduroys. He wouldn't look at me, and wouldn't look up. He smoothed the wales of his pant legs with the butt of his hand, pushing it forward like a snow shovel.

The lawyer stared out the window, ripped a bit of nail from his thumb, took it from his mouth, and pocketed it. "He won't listen to me," I told him. "You have to do it. She trusted you to do exactly what she wanted after she died. And she wanted to remain dead. No heroic measures. No feeding tubes or machines. Dead. Dead dead."

"I don't think I can do anything. I don't think this is even my area." Our lawyer pointed out the window, turned his back to us and away from his desk. We heard a quiet sniffle.

"Look at this. You're making the lawyer cry, Dad," I said.

"Hay fever," our lawyer swore, turning back and grabbing a tissue from a box on his desk. "It's just hay fever."

o

Dad drove us home, with Saxophone Lung motionless in the backseat. (We don't want her to sit up front and she never asks.) Glory was in my lap still straining her neck to the window, so I rolled it down a little more. The town drifted by, a fall day wasting into dusk, the small burning piles of leaves blooming orange in every front yard. It was going to get cold, soon, and the snow fall and fall into it reached our hips. From sky to horizon to the ground below—all would be white.

I couldn't look at my dad. I watched Glory watch the streets pass as we headed home. Then another driver, Wisconsin plates, cut us off and Dad laid on the horn. I yelled, "Dad!" He sped up, got right behind the car, and honked again and again. We heard a flat note from the back seat.

And then, a whistle. A whistling came from my mother's ears, playing along with the flat note that whined, muffled, in her chest. I looked in the rearview mirror and saw her struggling to keep her mouth closed. Her belly was expanding, pressing out against her pink sweatshirt. She shook her head rapidly, but would not open her mouth. She was sucking air in, and not letting it out. Her belly pressed more, distending. "Oh, God, let it out, mom," I said. But she kept expanding, and clamped her hands over her mouth.

I ducked. Dad hit the brakes and pulled us over to the side of the street. There was a bang, and the interior of the car was showered in mud, clay, and powder. And the objects. They whumped against the seat. Metal zippers, jewelry, and beads clinked against windows. The saxophone bounced off Dad's headrest and fell to the carpet.

My dad cursed. I uncovered Glory, who was whimpering and shaking in my arms. Dad looked at me and pursed his lips and blew out through his nose. Dust settled on his hair and eyebrows. I grabbed paper towels and glass cleaner from the bucket in front of me, unbuckled my seat belt and climbed in back to clean the mess from the rear window while my father wiped the windshield with his handkerchief and searched for a nearby place to park. He chose a bank parking lot. The bank was closed and the lot was empty. He leashed Glory and walked her to a nearby tree while I worked to get the windows clean enough for us to drive home.

I made a pile of my mother's clothes and sat it on the backseat. There was the saxophone, a beaded coin purse, a pocket watch—all the things that had been in this mother. I found my missing library card. And her wedding ring, which had rolled under the driver's seat. I wrapped her wedding ring up in a clean paper towel, and handed it to my dad when he had returned from Glory's walk. He put the ring in his pocket, and started the car. I sat down and put the bucket, filled with the larger scraps of clay, in front of me. Glory returned to my lap.

Back at the house, dad went down to the creek wearing a cracked pair of leather gloves and muddy overalls. He was going down to gather the clay for a replacement. When one mother went down, Dad liked to make another, to keep the number of replacements at four. Always four. "In case of something catastrophic," he said.

There's a small drop-off behind the house, a wall of clay. The roots of the trees at the edge of the bluff stick out more and more with every mother my dad makes.

I grabbed the mail. A couple of bills, overdue. Mine. This semester's catalog from Northern Michigan University had arrived. In my room, I shelved it with the others. I had a collection going, every new catalog for the last ten years.

There was a message on the answering machine from my boss, so after I finished a second, more thorough cleanout of the car, I decided to go to work and shelve books for a few hours. As I gathered my gloves and helmet from my room, the light barely over the bottom edge of the window, the gray dusk made a shadowy stage set of the trees. My father was below, working with a shovel, humming tunelessly, and the wheels of the wheelbarrow squeaked in rhythm.

I rolled up my pant leg and hugged it with a reflective Velcro strap on my right cuff to keep it from catching on the chain. My front and rear lights blinked, the front a quick flash on off on off, the back a series of three red lights in a random pattern. Like the fingers of a musician moving on the valves of a trumpet, a jazz musician playing, improvising—that's what the lights look like to me. Like Booker Little's fingers, maybe. If I could play, I'd record the flashing lights, transcribe the pattern, and practice with it, just to hear what it sounds like. If that would work. Frankly, I don't even know if that would work.

By the time I was ready to go, my dad was in the garage, building a mother. The door was cracked open. "I'm going in to work for a while," I told him. My father grunted. He was kneading the clay on the workbench, a large piece that looked to be the torso. He usually starts forming the body at the torso. A hot water bottle, the coin purse, and the saxophone were waiting next to him.

By bicycle, work is twenty minutes away. There's a nice, paved trail all the way so I don't have to worry about cars—just Marquette's hills. But it's downhill there, uphill back. Other cyclists and joggers are my only obstacles. When I see someone, I use the bell on my handlebars to tell them I'm approaching. I pull back the hammer, and let go and it rings out with a single, clear, clean chime. I only need it for joggers, though. I rarely pass other cyclists, as I ride to work in no real hurry. My boss's book and record shop, Baraga Books and More, is open all night.

He was listening to that Mal Waldron record I like. When I first came into the shop, he offered me a job because I told him I liked the tune that was playing. The word tune is what got him. "Real jazz fans call them tunes," he said. I told him I really didn't know much about jazz, but he said it didn't matter. I was a natural. I said I wasn't sleeping much because of my family. He told me he could use a shelver who didn't sleep much. I was happy to find a place to go at night that wasn't another bar.

"What's wrong with your family," he asked.

"My mom died, and my father won't let her go," I told him.

"Oh, I know what that's like. Your situation is exactly like what happened with my dad," he said.

"Yeah," I said. "I doubt it."

It was sudden: one day there, next day gone. Something in Mom's brain popped, and she was gone. I was 18, about to graduate. Dad was "away for a while to sort some things out." Mom was folding laundry on the floor, watching TV, with Glory jumping around and unfolding warm towels and pillowcases. It was just a coincidence that this happened on the day of the week Dad called to update us on his sorting-things-out progress. He might have missed the funeral, otherwise.

The church bathroom was small. It had two side-by-side stalls. Dad came in, I was already there, and he locked the door behind him.

He said, "I appreciate that you haven't said anything to anyone about the situation with your mother and me."

"Sure thing," I said.

"Because I really think it would have complicated this more than it already is, you know," he said.

"Sure. Yeah, sure," I said. "We don't want this any more complicated."

"I guess," he said, "I'll be moving back in now. I can bring my stuff up out of the basement."

I zipped up my pants and went to the sink to wash my hands.

"You think that'd be okay?" he asked. "Me moving back in now?"

"Well, people have brought us all that ham, so I guess so," I said.

Dad was standing in front of the door. "It's okay with you, though," he said, "if I move back in?"

"Oh, yeah," I said. "We can be one big happy family again."

I pushed past him. He flinched when I got close. He smelled like Old Spice and red wine. The organ was starting to hum from the sanctuary.

I like shelving, even though sometimes I find myself singing the alphabet song. I like listening to the music my boss plays, asking him who the musicians are. He tells stories about them. "I saw Eric Dolphy once, with Roy Haynes, and it was the first time it ever occurred to me that music could be serious and funny at the same time. In the middle of Dolphy's solo, I busted up. I don't remember what it was, but I swear the guy told a joke— with his flute!"

I've developed a bad case of shelver's knee. I've had to put patches on the right knees of all my jeans, because I lean on the right knee when I shelve low. I wore holes into a couple of pairs before I learned this trick.

I shelved for a couple of hours, and stopped when I picked up a book called *How to Disagree Without Arguing, Or At Least Argue Without Yelling.*

It was raining outside. The door opened and I could smell it.

If not for the bookshop, I'd have been home watching late-night talk shows. Before I'd found this place, and after I got sick of sitting on barstools, I was spending my evenings drinking beer and watching Morton Downey, Jr. on TV. My father started buying Hamm's in cases for me, because I was finishing all his good stuff too quickly. He told me the Hamm's was for when I wanted to drink in bulk.

Morton yelled, "Zip it!" at his guests, and I drifted in and out of sleep. The guests did their best, trying to act more unreasonable than they usually would, just to keep up with him. His audience hooted, wild and intense. Someone in the crowd walked up to the microphone and called a Middle Eastern guest a raghead and a camel jockey. The guest responded by calling him another fat American, but appeared embarrassed doing so.

I turned to find my mother's eyes on me in the flickering light of the television. They were shiny glass marbles. She was standing at the bottom of the steps. I nearly yelped. "How long have you been down here?" I said.

She stared at me. Then she turned and shuffled back up the stairs to her bedroom, coins jingling in her abdomen as she took the stairs. It was the model I called Change Purse Kidney. How had I not heard her coming down the stairs?

No matter which model, she spent her nights sitting in a rocking chair, waiting for dawn to enter the window. Glory slept in Mom's room, on her old bed, ignoring—as she always did—the fake in the chair. The mothers never scratched behind Glory's ear, never patted her belly, and I don't think Glory would have let them if one tried.

I started going out every night after I saw my father remaking my mother for the first time. This was after I had caused the first four or so to explode with screams of 1) fear at her return from the dead, 2) disbelief that clay could move and appear alive, 3) anger at my dad for causing this to happen, and 4) exasperation with my dad for continuing to build them. This was when we discovered all this "speak quietly and carefully around the mothers, or they will self-destruct" stuff.

While he works, he won't let me into the shed, but I watch through a small, dirty window. It takes about a week to sculpt her from clay. He fills her chest with things he finds in the basement, things shaped like human organs. In the garage, he has a female anatomy poster. The partially skinned woman—open to show her lungs, and her heart, and her stomach—has blue eyes, and she looks tired. Her eyelids, still there, are heavy. Her right hand and arm, ungloved of its skin, is resting on her right shoulder. She has brown hair in a ponytail falling down behind her.

He makes mothers to replace the ones we lose. He sometimes sits at his old drafting table, working out plans for new models. Gone are the days of the Popsicle stick skeletons, glued together with Elmer's. Now, a travel toiletries case for a liver. Now, Clarinet Throat.

We still do the dishes together, my mother and I—just like we used to. I wash and she dries, rubber gloves on her hands so her fingers don't melt on the warm film of water that covers each dish. We do it in silence. It is best to do everything in silence, or with music playing. She likes jazz standards, ballads. But she can no longer listen to the music of her youth. Polka now puts her on edge.

There was one time when we didn't work in silence. I was saying that I was thinking of finally going to college. I had been looking at the applications on my desk. I was nearly 30, and it felt like it was time to leave the nest.

I was lingering on a black plate, drawing with my fingertips in the soap bubbles; four intertwined figure eights. "But, I'll visit a lot," I said. She was shaking, bloating, dropped the dish in her hand, and blew. A piece of her torso knocked me sideways and to the floor. She gave me a black eye. "Oh, Mom," I said. I picked up her ring. "What are we going to do?"

Her clarinet was on the floor. So were the missing keys to the tool shed.

Dad stood in the doorway to the kitchen. I dropped the ring in his hand, and headed to the laundry room for a bucket and ammonia.

So, now I don't say anything at all. I draw on the plates, and she dries. When I finish, I pat her shoulder and head out to work.

I asked my boss whom we were listening to.

"Art Pepper and Chet Baker," he said. "*Playboys*. The one with the woman holding the puppets across her bare breasts on the cover.

"You know Chet Baker never practiced," said my boss. "Not once. He was just a pure player. And, boy, was he hot. Good-looking young man. Until he lost all his teeth."

I was sitting on a step stool, going through the Classics shelf, making sure everything was in alphabetical order. I was reorganizing Cicero, whom someone had left all out of whack.

After, I went over to a pile of polka records my boss had purchased earlier that evening. "There's something in there you might be interested in," he said. Instead of asking which, though, I just began to alphabetize.

And soon, there she was. In the middle of the stack was an album by The Marquette Polka Pets. I knew all about The Marquette Polka Pets.

It was a mid-60's recording on a small label. The band was all-girl. They wore skimpy, cheesecake outfits and cat-ear headbands. Mom was standing behind the drummer, tenor saxophone on a strap around her neck. On the back, it said she played tenor sax and clarinet for the band. "I saw them," my boss said. "Way back when. Your mom had this trick where she would play the saxophone and clarinet at the same time for a whole song. It was pretty impressive. The guys loved them."

They had fake fur cattails. The Pets played a show for the insurance company where my dad worked. He went to see them a lot, after that. He even learned the basic steps so he could dance.

He seemed to her to be a good man, so she went out with him for a while. Then, for the same reason, she agreed to marry him.

The photo albums have lots of photos of her in front of things. And next to each photo is a photo of him in front of things. If only Dad had purchased a tripod at some point. They do, however, have matching clothes in many of the pictures. And Dad always seems to be standing a couple of feet away from where Mom was standing in the first photo. A razor blade, some glue, and a steady hand could do wonders for the memory of their relationship.

My father starts the detail work at her feet, and works his way up. Me, I'd probably start with the face and work down. This is, in a nutshell, the difference between my father and me. I begin a project full of hope and optimism, and end it rushing, wanting to move on to whatever is next. His enthusiasm for creating builds as he works. If I made a mother feet-first, they would have perfectly formed toes, ankles, and legs, but by the time I got to the face, I'd cut corners. Mother would come to life with the soft, featureless face of a mannequin. My father's feet may be a serviceable approximation, but his face is lovely and accurate—even when it scatters in pieces across a room.

My father's not a shaman. He's not a magician. He's not a priest. He's a retired actuary. Nothing in his past explains how he is able to do this. He has no connection to anything beyond what has always been our comfortable, explainable reality. No ties to the occult. No special connection to God.

Not that I know of.

He's standing nearby, and tying her sneaker. "Anna," he says, "I'm so angry at you. I can't believe you died without ever forgiving me. You're a very selfish woman, Anna. A very selfish woman, and I can't forgive you, either."

He slips the ring into her mouth. And she turns her head down to him. She's back again.

He walks back to the house, past me. I don't even try to hide. She follows. He holds the door for her, and they go into the house.

This is what I am going to do, so help me God. I will fight with my dad tomorrow. Or perhaps the next day. I will fight with him with my mother standing right there. And she'll go off again.

I'll get to the ring first. I won't give it back. I'm taller than my dad, now, so I will stand there, holding the ring up as high as I can, holding the ring up as he struggles to get me to give it to him.

And I won't give it to him. I'll keep the ring held over his reach as long as I need to. Until he gives up, and slumps to the floor. And I'll keep holding it up there. He won't get it back from me. I'll stand there forever, if I have to.

college

"Where are you?"

"You know where I am."

"Are you in your dorm room?"

"Yes."

"Describe it."

"It's a room."

"Describe the room. Everything. Tell me everything about the room."

"It's a room. Bed. Window. Desk. Door. Bathroom."

"No. Tell me. Tell me more. I need you to tell me details."

"Why?"

"Because I don't know where you are."

"I'm in my dorm room. In Ann Arbor. In Michigan. In the USA. On planet Earth. In our solar system. In the Milky Way galaxy."

"Don't make fun. Tell me about the room."

"Why?"

"The room. I want to see it."

"See it?"

"You're in a submarine to me right now. Under the Antarctic. You're lost on the Moon. I can't see where you are. I can't see you."

"Are you still high?"

"Tell me what the room looks like."

"Stone Roses, I think. Public Enemy. *Master of Puppets*."

"The tape I made you?"

"Yeah, that's there."

"When are you coming home?"

"Spring break."

"Before?"

"No. My car won't make it. I'll break down in Sault Ste. Marie."

"I'll come get you."

"They won't let you."

"I'll steal their car."

"They watch you."

"I'll take another car. I'll just take one."

"You know you won't. You're afraid to drive."

"I won't be."

"I should sleep now."

"Don't. Don't hang up."

"I have to go."

"Don't hang up."

"I really have to go. I love you."

"Please don't hang up."

"Jessi."

"Please. A little more. Tell me a little more."

"Honey."

"Tell me about what you see when you look out the window."

"I'm going. You called at 11."

"Tell me. I want to see you."

"Let me sleep."

"Don't hang up. Please."

"I'm going."

"Don't hang up. Just—"

happy
rock

"Fuck this town," she says. "I hate this town."

The new soda machine has extra large buttons. Lodi thinks it looks like the interface a trained chimp would use to fly a rocket ship. "Big buttons. Hit the red one, rocket goes up. Hit the blue one, rocket comes down. Hit the green one, hatch opens up, and space chimp gets a banana. Gets a parade around New York. Gets to meet the president. Gets to retire. Simple."

"Because we're like trained monkeys is why you say that, right? The people who work here, we're all like trained monkeys. You're making the point that, you know, management thinks we're all trained monkeys and anyone could do our jobs," says a man, a coworker whom Lodi has been introduced to once or twice and sees every single day, but whose name she, frankly, has completely forgotten. He is smiling and he is nodding slowly at her. "That's funny. That's pretty funny."

She thinks probably he is coming on to her or is going to come on to her if the conversation continues, so she decides not to get into the whole chimp-not-monkey conversation someone should have gotten into with him in grade school or earlier. Lodi waits for Diana to meet her at the soda machine before she goes on. Diana is walking slowly, reading something in a magazine, her head down. She is tall and thin, and her hair reaches down her back almost to her waist in a style Lodi likes to refer to as "Christian-splinter-group-chic." They are in the break room, which is overwhelmingly beige and too small for the number of people who work at the bank. The male coworker has left, slinked off, perhaps headed to the bathroom. Someone is asleep on an old brown leather couch in the corner, his nose lightly whistling, but otherwise, the tables are empty. The comfortable chairs are empty. The room is mostly empty. Just Lodi, and Diana, who is microwaving something—soup maybe—the whistler, and the man whose name Lodi has forgotten. He is wearing khaki pants and running shoes, a look Lodi despises. By the transitive process, Lodi despises the man. He has glasses, but otherwise his face is indistinct and practically invisible.

"Also, on the old soda machines, you had just the logo of the soda," she says. She and Diana are finding a seat at the table, and Diana is flipping through the magazine. There is a woman with a huge number of children on the cover of the magazine. She looks pleased with herself. "Or before that, machines just had little placards with the name of the product, but now it's a picture of the can, and a familiar color scheme. Dark blue is regular cola, light blue is diet."

"Because it's less like a real cola?" says Diana, looking up from her magazine. "Some of the blue has been leeched out of it, and now it's light blue."

"Exactly," says Lodi. "The blueness represents the amount of real 'colaness' of the product. And green, the universal short hand for lemon-lime sodas."

"From words to pictures. It's like they think we're devolving," says Diana. "Our brains are getting simpler."

"I for one have enough to think about in my day," says Lodi, "and appreciate that they are allowing me to make my snack choices based on pictograms."

Diana and Lodi laugh, and return to their stations at the bank. Diana works in the Credit Department. Lodi is a teller.

Lodi took the job a year ago, and has refused to apply for a transfer to positions with more responsibility whenever they have come up. She will leave the bank and return to Chicago—where she lived for three years with her now ex-fiancé Nico, and waited tables in the Greek restaurant his parents owned—any month now, she thinks. Any month now.

An hour passes uneventfully, and Diana sends Lodi a text message, asking if they are going out tonight. Lodi responds: "Of course." It is Tuesday. Lodi and Diana go out after work on Tuesdays and Thursdays for drinks. Friends—well, coworkers whose tone in conversation and interest in the lives of the girls approximates something that some might call friendship—are puzzled by this schedule.

"Why not on Fridays and Saturdays? Why go out on a work night."

"Why waste a perfectly good Saturday or Sunday recovering from a hangover?" says Lodi.

"Work is already as uncomfortable as it can be," says Diana. "Being hung over can't possibly make it any worse." This tends to make so much sense to their coworkers that the coworkers think maybe they will tag along. Lodi and Diana very quietly discourage this, and eventually, said coworkers tell them they have something else they need to do that night. Something they forgot about. "But next time?" they say. "Definitely. Definitely." And it never comes up again.

Lodi and Diana text message one another for the dwindling hours of work. Lacking opportunities to showcase their abilities as customer service representatives, they focus their attention on a vibrating and buzzing device of plastic and aluminum in the palms of their hands. Lodi has a tiny pair of earphones, and surreptitiously slips them in under her long brown hair, the cord trailing in through the sleeves of the long white and pintucked blue shirt which she wears on Tuesdays. She can get away with listening to music on her phone if she stays ever so slightly on guard, as her coworkers and employers are ever so genuinely disinterested in the day to day operations of the business at levels below or parallel to their own.

An old man approaches the counter, and Lodi uses the volume wheel of the phone in her hand to turn her music down.

"Hi, sir. My name's Laura. How can I help you?" Lodi says. Lodi hears herself say Laura, because in fact she is Laura, but as the name spins in her mind, she changes it back to Lodi. She knows what the old man wants. He has a jar of change in his hands.

"Hello, dear," says the old man, who has a fringe of white hair over his ears, and patches of dry skin under his eyes. "Can you change this into folding money for me?"

"Of course," she says, reaching over the counter for the jar. She walks the jar in back to the coin counter, uncorks it, and turns the contents into the metal funnel. When a manager approaches her, she yanks hard on the phone in her hand, and pulls the earphones from her ears and in through the collar of her shirt. Her ear is sore from repeated yanks at her earphones. She crinkles her nose a little. She wonders how long it will take to get used to this—to maybe grow some sort of callus.

"Almost time to go home, eh Laura?" he says.

"Sure is," says Lodi.

"Sure is," he says. And he stands in front of her for a moment, his mouth slightly open, his eyes unfocused, his fingers scratching a manila folder.

"Only Tuesday, though," Lodi says.

"Yes. Tuesday. That's right!" says the manager. He laughs.

"That can only mean one thing," says Lodi. The manager's eyebrows go up a little, and he leans in to Lodi. "Tomorrow is Wednesday," she says.

"Well, I guess I can't argue with that," he says.

Lodi's coins have been counted, and she checks the total, and writes it on a slip of white paper with a short pencil. There is a box of short pencils on the machine. There are boxes of short pencils everywhere in the bank.

It's eleven dollars and thirty-eight cents. Lodi walks back to the counter and counts out the money for the old man.

"Thanks, dear," he says.

"You're very welcome," she says.

"Are you new here?" says the old man. "I come here every other week or so, and I don't think I've ever seen you before."

"No, I've been here," she says. "I've waited on you, I think."

"Oh," says the old man. "I'm sorry. Well, I'll remember you next time."

"Thanks," she says. "I'm sure you will. And I'll remember you, too."

"I will, though," says the old man. "I noticed as you walked away that you have a really nice butt. A little thicker. That's how I like them."

Lodi watches the old man as he walks away.

Lodi's phone vibrates, and she looks at it to see a message from Diana. "$13?" it says.

For some reason, they go to the bar called Bleachers again. Not Doc's or Schooners or The Main Street Tap. It seems like the only age-appropriate bar in town, even if the crowd only serves to annoy Lodi in that everyone there seems to be someone she knows from high school.

In Chicago, her ex, Nicky, is probably out, probably with a Greek girl, like his mother always wanted him to date instead of Lodi. Nicky's new girl has family in town, and he is polite to a fault to the girl's mother and to her father, flirty—but not overbearing and creepy—with her teenage sister. She maybe has a baby by another man—a little boy. One or two years of age, possibly. Nicky is patient with the child, but has gotten to the point where he feels comfortable punishing him if he talks back to his mother, or disobeys her.

Diana goes to the bathroom. "Off to drain the lizard," she says. Lodi, eyes soft and red, laughs and turns in to her elbows, hunkers down, and watches the light flash and strobe on the ice in her glass.

The bartender went to high school with Lodi. "Go Gladstone Braves," she says every time he wipes up the condensation and spills on the bar in front of her. He smiles a friendly smile every time. He was a JV running back. He says he's now going to Bay de Noc Community College and getting an associate's degree in something, but Lodi doesn't hear what. He remembers Lodi's family and asks after them: How's your mother? How's your father? How's your brother? Still in Iraq?

Everyone is fine, and everyone's in touch. "Mike called from Qatar," she says. "They gave him a pass, and sent him to this big building that looks like a warehouse outside. Inside it looks like a Vegas nightclub. They only allow him three drinks a night and never any liquor. He's drinking wine now because it's stronger."

"Have one for him, then?" says the bartender

"Yes," Lodi says. Diana has returned and is sitting next to her again. "I'd like the strongest shot you've got."

"The strongest shot you've got," echoes Diana.

"The strongest shot you've got," says Lodi. And then both of them are saying it together, and their four fists are pounding on the bar. "The strongest shot you've got. The strongest shot you've got."

The bartender pulls a bottle from the top shelf and fills two shot glasses. "On the house," he says. "One hundred proof. I'm not supposed to serve it without a mixer, but just this once. For your brother. On the house."

"Go Braves," Lodi says.

Lodi tells Diana that in Chicago they are wearing sack dresses, and they are wearing thin, braided leather headbands. They are wearing hot pink, and they are wearing the brims of their baseball caps flat and turned up again. They are wearing paper denim, and they have jeans that flatten their asses out entirely. And they are staying out all night and they are doing cocaine again.

"What a magical time it must be," says Diana.

"If you only knew," says Lodi.

Diana reaches into her purse and pulls out cigarettes. She shakes two free, and they wait for the man behind the bar to notice. They wait for him to offer to light their cigarettes for them. When this does not happen quite quickly enough, Diana says: "Richard, do you see what the two lovely young ladies at the bar are holding?"

The bartender says: "I do. I do see what the two lovely young ladies at the bar are holding." He comes over with a pack of matches, bends one out of the booklet without breaking it off, flicks it against the coarse band with his thumb, and holds the pack out. Diana and Lodi lean in and light their cigarettes at the same time. When they lean back, the bartender holds the pack up, and snaps his fingers next to it, one finger flicking the cardboard extinguishing the flame in the jerk. He drops it next to them on the counter, and moves down to talk with a man about his age, a man drinking beer and wearing a Packers jacket.

"That was," says Diana.

"Quite impressive," says Lodi.

"Quite impressive," says Diana.

"And masculine," says Lodi. "Let's not forget masculine."

"Extremely masculine," says Diana.

"I might be a little moist," says Lodi.

"In her private area," says Diana.

"My super-private girl area," says Lodi.

Diana turns her chair to Lodi, and turns Lodi's chair to her. She grabs Lodi by the shoulders and looks at her. Lodi looks back. "But, mostly, let's," she says, "not forget masculine, shall we?"

Lodi says, "No, no. Never. We'll never forget that. We must never forget." She turns back to the bar, and, with the back of her hand, knocks her drink over. The shot spills, runs the length of the empty bar to the end, and trickles over the side.

"Let's not," says Lodi, picking up the pack of matches. "Let's not ever." Lodi strikes a match. She uses it to light all the remaining matches.

Lodi holds the pack over the pooling alcohol.

Lodi's brother is on his second tour. People seem to be shooting at him less and less these days. This is not really as comforting as he thought it might be when he was praying that people would shoot at him less. He has learned to say hello, and he has learned to say thank you, and he has learned to say stop in Arabic. He spends a lot of time in armored vehicles that could do with more armoring. He has gotten over his motion sickness. When he is at work, his feet hurt.

He talks to Lodi whenever he can, which is not often. He talks to his parents, too, but he seems to prefer talking to Lodi. "Lodi," he says, "I miss you."

"You're the only one who calls me that," she says. "Why do you call me that?"

There are a couple dozen other questions she has but she refuses to ask them.

"Do you miss Nicky?" he says.

"Not in the least," she says. "Not even a little."

He tells her that he was out on patrol one day and saw a little boy who had collected shell casings. The little boy held them in his palms and was looking at them. Lodi's brother knelt in front of the boy and looked, too.

He made a gesture, like, *May I?* and the little boy made a gesture of agreement. He took the shell casings from the boy and set them up against the wall in a triangle, like a bowling alley, and he looked around for a small, round rock. When he found one, he walked a few paces from the wall and dug a line in the dirt with his boot. Then he did a little underhand toss that rolled the rock at the shell casings. A few fell over but not all of them. He walked back and set up the casings again, walked back to the line, and motioned for the boy to come over to him. Then he taught the boy to bowl. "I guess he was eight or nine. Hell, I don't know, though. Maybe 12. I can never tell."

Lodi drops the flaming pack into the spill, and watches a blue flame appear, and cross the bar, and titter and stumble and wither and wave. Diana has turned away to look out the window. Her back is aflutter with light.

eugenius

When this place belonged to his great grandparents, there were half as many houses as there are now, half as many streets. The little building that now serves as the elementary school was the high school. The hardware store was open and doing business six days a week—not like now, when it is filled with old merchandise covered in dust and the "Closed temporarily due to health," sign hasn't moved from the window in years and years. There were two churches and a funeral home—now there are two more churches, but no additional funeral homes. There were only a few dozen houses with basements—one story, and many were in the process of having the wood covered with aluminum siding. Now there are two and three story homes. The beach had no lifeguards, and the grocery store had a local owner—but this had not changed. Eugene's grandfather worked at the bakery, and he was married, and he was happy, and he was in love. Eugene also worked at the bakery, and he was happy—mostly—and he was in love. This was their house, a one-story house, still clapboard.

The morning it occurred to him to photograph his Marie, it was cold and early February. Saturday, so he was not expected at work. She was asleep beside him, just a few minutes away from being woken up by the buzzing of their alarm clock. He always beat the thing to waking up. A little bit of light had tumbled in through a space between the curtain and the window of their bedroom, and it was settled on the curve of her cheek, just below her eye, not quite to the point when it would flash red inside her lid and startle her, shift her, wake her. Eugene turned from his stomach to his side, and looked at Marie. The muscles of her face were soft. There were no wrinkles, no smile or frown, just a steady, round, passive face. They had received a camera as an anniversary gift, had taken it with them to Mackinaw Island for the honeymoon, but hadn't used it, and it was still in its box. That was years ago, and Eugene thought probably the film had gone south, though he wasn't precisely sure how film went south, or even if, in fact, it did go south, or what, precisely it meant for film to go south. That was the word that had occurred to him. It just seemed to him likely that film did, after time, go south, and that the old film that came with the camera had gone that way.

But he should take photos of Marie when she woke up. He thought it inappropriate to take photos of her asleep. As he watched his Marie sleep, he thought about what he would use as a backdrop (one of the thick, lined cotton drapes with a golden lily pattern), and how he would ask her to pose (sitting on the floor, leaning forward, her knees up and her hands clasped around them, smiling and looking at him, in one of her church dresses), and what they would do with her hair (put it up in a clasp, one with beads and silver edges). He reached over to the night table, and grabbed a tissue—the only blank paper available to him—and decided that it was important for him to buy a notebook later in the day that he could use to write in and sketch in early in the morning when he wasn't ready to get out of bed because it was chilly, or because he did not want to wake Marie by thumping around on the bedroom's hardwood floors. There was a pencil next to a book. (Eugene was reading a geology textbook that a friend had given him, and he was marking it up.) He did a rough sketch of the pose, and thought that he was better at sketching than he had assumed he would be. He had never really tried.

Marie woke up. "Can I take your picture?" Eugene said.

"I suppose that would be fine," Marie said, after a quiet moment.

"Okay," he said. "I'll go pick out a dress. You get ready."

"Get ready?" she said.

"Yeah," he said. "A nice photo. In makeup. Is that okay?"

"Why?" she said.

"I would really like it," he said. When Eugene smiled, Marie decided to do it. She got ready. She washed her face, and put on powder. She put on lipstick. She found a dress waiting for her when she left the washroom. She found the house dark. She found Eugene setting up the camera on a chair. "We should get a tripod soon, I think," he said. She agreed that they should get a tripod. It made Eugene happy that she understood that they would need a tripod.

In the first few photos, Marie was not comfortable, but she did her best. Marie looked at the images, after they had been developed, and saw stiffness, unnaturalness. But Eugene had persisted. He moved a hair, he bent a wrist, he smoothed a wrinkle in a dress. He shifted light—a lamp denuded of its shade—to move shadows across her face. Marie even allowed him to trim her hair a little where the ends were loose.

"I don't think I like this," Marie said.

"Yes you do," he said.

"I do?" she said.

"Of course," he said. "Of course you do."

Marie was unsure. "You will like it," Eugene said. "I can tell."

"How can you tell," Marie said.

"I can see it in the prints," he said. "I can see you slowly liking it."

"Show me," she said.

Eugene showed her the photos, and pointed to places on her face, places that were stiff in an early photo, and looser in the very next shot. She could see that it was dawning on her to enjoy what was happening.

"Do you see it?" said Eugene.

"You know what? I do," she said. "I actually see it. Right—there," she said, grabbing two pictures and flipping from one to the next. "The eyes, see?"

"Yup," he said. "That's what I was saying. It's all right there."

He bought photo magazines at the drug store. Some were general interest, and featured photo spreads of stars at home. Some were what his manager referred to as "gentlemen's magazines" and made his coworkers blanch when he read them in over lunch in the kitchen seated on a pile of bags of flour.

"Could you not look at those here?" said his manager. He had also been his father's manager.

"I'm researching," said Eugene.

"Why would you need to do that kind of research," said another baker. "Don't you have a wife at home? Are you not getting enough of it?"

"I'm researching," said Eugene.

"Research in the bathroom," said the manager. "Research out of sight."

The photos changed the more he looked at the photos in the magazines and thought about them. When Eugene promised to learn how to develop photos on his own and began work on a dark room in the basement, Marie agreed to remove her shirt for him. They used stark backgrounds, empty walls, and brighter lights to create sharp lines of contrast, between her body and the background. But only for a little while.

Soon Marie said: "I miss the patterns. Can we have the drapes back?"

And Eugene said: "You're right. We need the backgrounds again. And this." He produced a rope of fake pearls. They cinched them under her breasts, coiled them around her neck.

Marie said: "This seems wrong, though. I don't like being tied."

Eugene agreed, and they never used the pearls around her neck or over her wrists, or around her ankles again. A blindfold, now and then, was as risqué, as dangerous as they got.

Eugene went to the Carnegie Library, and got a book on photography. He saw a picture of a girl standing next to a girl who was also her. Not twins; the same girl. He read a chapter on double exposures. Marie sat for him, turned her neck left first, and right a few seconds later, two faces both smiling in profile, a crown of tinfoil on her head, a necklace of glass beads around her neck, an ostrich feather at her neck.

In the kitchen he hung a photo of himself in his favorite chair. He was frowning. Above him floated Marie's eye. He called it "She's Away," and wrote it in ink on the photo's white border.

He kept every negative. Even if the photo was overexposed, even if the image was little more than blur and fuzz and light and shadow, even if all that could be made out was the gentle tip of Marie's nose, turned toward a washed out field of gray, a blur of eyelash and bird-feather headdress. Even if there was nothing there, nothing at all no matter how hard you squinted, he kept it in a box in his studio.

They ate dinner together at the kitchen table, listening to the radio. The strongest signal was a station that played polkas, so they kept the music low. Marie was still learning to cook, and Eugene got a discount at the bakery, so rolls and chicken were the meal five days a week.

"I love chicken," said Eugene. "You can cook it every night." And she very nearly did. Roasted chicken and rolls with a little butter. Eugene stacked the bones. "Don't throw those away," he said. "I'd like to wash them and hang on to them."

Eugene dropped the bones into a pan filled with bleach and left them in the basement for a couple of days. When they had gone white and clean, he set them on a towel to dry, and went to the hardware store for paint. "Gold. I'd like a can of gold paint. And not flat," he said. "Shiny."

"What do you want shiny gold paint for?" asked the clerk. "What call does anyone have for shiny gold paint?" The clerk called over the manager and, as Eugene paid for the paint, they together wondered aloud as to the reasons a man would buy shiny gold paint.

"Why precisely," said Eugene," do you carry it if you don't expect to sell it?"

"Well, for a woman, maybe," said the store manager. "I mean, it's shiny. Shiny?"

Eugene put the paint in a bag, as the clerk seemed too involved in conversation with the manager to do so for him, and left the hardware store. He walked home down Delta Avenue, past a bar and a restaurant. It was late afternoon, and there was a rippled, thin cloud in the sky that reminded Eugene of gauzy material he had seen, and considered draping over Marie while she sat naked on their rocking chair, long with thin chains threaded through her earrings and braided into the supports at the chair's arms. She had objected to this pose. The wooden chair, she said, was too cold without a pillow beneath her. And he refused to let a pillow ruin the image he had in his head. It was the first time that a disagreement had led to him abandoning his inspiration.

It was the first time they had fought about art.

"We're fighting about art!" he said.

"We are?" she said.

"We are!" he said.

"You know what," she said. "We are. We are fighting about art. Me and my little Eugenius." It was the first time she called him that. The very first of many.

At home, he dipped a kitchen sponge in the gold paint, and used it to wipe color across the chicken bones. It was after dinner and Marie took a walk down to the beach.

"Would you come with?" she said.

"Not tonight," he said. "I have some art to make." He dipped the sponge in the paint, and covered each bone. He left little spots, though, where the bones would rest as they dried. He covered the legs and the wings, the ribs and the wishbones, the leftovers of the many chicken dinners he had eaten over the last few months. He set them to dry, a rotating fan sweeping back and forth over each delicate bone that sat on his workbench on a long section of paper towel.

"I would like you to come with me," she said. "It's a beautiful night."

"Tomorrow, maybe," he said. "Tonight, I need to paint these chicken bones gold."

At the beach, Marie saw her neighbor with their young

daughter. The little girl ran up to Marie to say hello, towing mother behind with an invisible cord. She had a stone and a shell in her hand. Marie asked to see the stone and the shell, and together they walked to the water. "Watch," said Marie. She dipped the end of the stone in the water, and it went from flat gray to dark and spotted like a little round, smoothed, limbless, headless leopard. The little girl smiled. She grabbed back the stone and dipped it, watched it change color, dried it off and watched it change back. Marie made small talk with the mother, but she thought about the shell she had pocketed. Eugene could use this, she thought.

When she returned home, it was dark, but Eugene was still in the basement, waiting for the paint on his bones to dry so he could turn them. "You should come up now and go to bed, don't you think?" Marie said.

"Soon. This one's almost dry," he said.

"But I have something for you," she said.

"Soon," he said.

"It's something you could use for your art," she said.

Eugene came up the stairs very quickly. Marie handed him the seashell. "You could do something with this, yeah?" she said.

"It's small," he said.

"Yes, but there are thousands of them, not five blocks away."

"Thousands," Eugene said.

"Thousands," Marie said. "And all of them are free, too."

"Thousands free," Eugene said, smiling.

"Thousands free," Marie said, smiling too. After that, Marie walked to the beach every night with a canvas bag. At first, she only grabbed shells. Soon, she picked up smoothed bits of broken glass and medium sized Petoskey stones, too. She washed them in the sink with a brush after each walk, and collected them in a bucket next to the kitchen sink. She chose a measuring cup for him to use as a scoop.

Two weeks later, Eugene bought an old lamp from a church rummage sale. It did not look to be in very good shape, but Eugene considered the venue at which it was being offered for sale, and felt confident it would work when plugged in and given a new light bulb. The church took light very seriously. He took the lamp to his workbench in the basement. Eugene had taken to dipping his chicken bones directly in the paint and hanging them from lines he had strung around the basement in simple webs. They hung down, stirred when bumped, rattled. They were attached by clothespins. Drips of gold paint dotted the concrete floor, but both Eugene and Marie had decided not to care. He used strong glue to attach a full set of ribs to the sides of the lamp, so they looked like the spines of a Chinese fan running up each side. He covered the base in seashells and bits of colored glass. When he brought it upstairs to show Marie— the very next day, new bulb already in the socket—he said: "You were right about the shells. And glass. We need more."

Marie pointed to the bucket, which in the last weeks had filled three quarters of the way up.

He made a small chair from the chicken bones. It was a rocking chair with curved, golden femurs as the rockers. It was only a couple of inches tall, and it sat on the sideboard next to the glass decanter (which was now covered in green and blue and brown and red bits of glass along its neck). He made a tower of ribs and wishbones, and placed a cat's eye marble at the very top. "This is our own Eiffel tower," he said. "For our city of love. Marie's Eiffel."

Marie was caught off-guard: "Eugene, I think what you just said could be considered romantic. This is an unexpected and delightful surprise."

After that, Eugene started to name all of his art, and used her name in every piece. Many of the photos became Marie Study This, or Marie Study That. Marie in Black Lace. Marie at the Beach with Candle. Marie Sublime Number One. Eugene went to the Carnegie Library and checked out books on art, studied the names, and used variations of them. But he rarely copied the designs. This was when he had started keeping a journal, and one day he wrote: I would not make a Marie Lisa, or anything. My own head is filled with too many ideas for me to need anyone else's.

To the great satisfaction of the clerk and manager at the hardware store, he bought a bag of cement, and a basin in which to mix it.

"Now that's more like it," the manager said.

He brought the concrete outside, and covered a birdbath with glass and shells and marbles. When it was finished, he called Marie to come outside, and asked her to fill a pitcher with water to bring with her. She did so. "Pour it in," he said. When she did, the gray Petoskey stones that lined the bottom turned dark and spotted like leopard hide. Marie ran to both the houses on either side of them, and grabbed the neighbors, but only after she had asked Eugene to dump out the water and dry the stones. The neighbors arrived—two wives, two husbands, three children— and Marie told them to look at the birdbath.

"Pour it in," she said. Eugene had refilled the pitcher, and poured water over the stones, changing them. "What do you think?" Marie said.

The neighbors said little, just a "That's nice," and a "Pretty neat." One asked where they had gotten the odd, ornate birdbath. Marie said: "My husband, the artist, made it. My Eugenius."

The neighbors looked at one another. "Nice," they said. "Nice," they agreed.

At the bakery, everyone wanted to know why Eugene was spending so much of his time just reading books. He was looking at art books and photography books in every spare moment. It seemed to them impractical, they said. "I'm an artist, now," Eugene told them. "I make art."

They suggested that, instead, he should consider making more rolls.

But at home there was a sign on the mailbox that said Eugene DeKeyser, Artist. Marie had made it. Eugene had added to it. Marie DeKeyser, Muse. The mailman, when first encountering the sign, knocked on the door and asked Marie about it. "I don't know if it's legal for me to deliver letters if they aren't addressed specifically to who is on the box. I think it might be against a federal law," he said. He also wondered if the titles were academic, if the DeKeysers had degrees nailed to their walls proving that they were earned appellations. After a short conversation, Marie found out that the mailman simply didn't know what a muse was, and feared the word might be offensive to public decency standards. Marie showed him a definition in the dictionary.

"Oh," he said. "I guess that's okay, then."

On the day after his birthday, Eugene asked for an extra day off a week at the bakery. Marie had purchased a set of oil paints for him. They came in the mail. It was late autumn. They cleaned the leaves from the birdbath every other day. The trim on the windows of the house was bright, shiny gold, and the hardware store had been forced to order larger cans of gold paint. Eugene had to put down a deposit, and swear that he would use all of it. The manager had personally walked him to the closest church so they could find a Bible on which the oath could be taken. Not finding a Bible, they used a hymnal.

"That's as good as anything else," said the hardware store manager. "Don't think you can just get away with not buying the paint because this is a hymnal instead of a Bible. It counts, too, in Jesus' eyes."

The paints arrived, but the company had forgotten to send the small brushes. Eugene was anxious to paint, but the hardware store was closed. Marie convinced Eugene to go for a walk with her so that they could think. On Delta Avenue, they stopped at a tavern called The Shanty. They ordered sandwiches and drinks: a cola for Eugene, a cocktail for Marie. Eugene asked the waitress if the restaurant had chicken bones it was willing to part with. (They didn't.) Marie stirred her drink with a tiny red straw.

When they got home, Eugene went back to the basement to look at the set of paints. Marie took her small red straw and his larger white and red-striped straw from her pocket. She went to the bathroom and, with a small pair of scissors, removed a lock of her hair. She split the lock into a small bundle and a large bundle, and took metal ring from a bracelet with a broken hasp from the drawer by her bed. She squeezed the ring at the end of the small straw, the smaller bundle of hair inside it.

"Genie," she said, coming down the steps. "Look. Brush."

Eugene had a piece of paper attached to a wooden board on the workbench, braced to make an easel. He was squeezing black paint onto his index finger and tracing a long, round shape on the paper, then drawing the end of a popsicle stick through the thick lines of paint. The stick pulled wisps of paint into the round shape, making a tunnel of grass or hair. Eugene turned to look. "Now we just need something round and metal for this straw," Marie said, bringing out the larger straw and larger bundle of her hair. "Any ideas?"

The next summer, the town had grown, but not all that much. The same churches and shops were open, though a new tavern had also appeared, and the beach now had a few more older people combing it, and a few more younger people staring at Bay de Noc from it. On July 4th, Marie's family came down from

Munising to visit their daughter and son-in-law for the first time in three years. They took a bus, and Eugene met them at the highway to help carry their bags.

"You look good," said Marie's father. "Where's Marie?"

"She's busy back at the house," said Eugene. "We have a surprise for you, and she wanted to get things ready there."

"It's about time we had grandchildren," said Marie's mother. "Finally the two of you have gotten to work."

"Now, we don't know that *that* is it, Franny," said Marie's father, his eyes a little gleamy. "The young man said a surprise." He winked at Eugene. "It could be nearly anything. Not just the blessing of a child."

Marie's mother put her hand on Eugene's shoulder and squeezed. "Mr. Lindstrom here was a wonderful father, even though he worried about it while I was pregnant. But he really took to it. You will, too. I feel certain of it." She left her hand on Eugene's shoulder all through the walk back to the house, and she pressed down, sometimes making it difficult for him to keep the suitcase in his hand. She told Eugene about the month before Marie's birth, when her husband disappeared for four days, out on a bender, sick and scared of having the responsibility of a child. "But he came right back after that four days. He came right back and he stayed with me. And he never said a word about it, though I knew what had happened.

"When Marie was born, he fell in love with her, and didn't leave her side for two weeks. Exhausted as I was, I had to get up and bring him food. He just sat by her crib in a chair, staring down at her. Wouldn't even go to work. But on a Monday, two weeks later, he went to work in the morning, and no one said anything. He sat down at his desk at the Bank and Trust, and never missed another day until he retired. He became a man. That's what will happen to you."

Eugene looked at Marie's father, who was rolling a cigarette in spry, wrinkled hands. He was ignoring his wife. They passed burned lawns, a rosebush, and a bathtub Madonna on their way to the house. They passed them without comment.

This is what Marie's parents saw when they arrived at the house: a low picket fence of yellow and eggshell blue; a house with gold trim and four sides with four different colors: lime green, brick red, dark blue, and shiny silver; a yard filled with sculptures, towers of resin-covered, golden chicken bones as tall as Marie and concrete mushrooms dotted with marbles, shells, and pieces of smoothed glass; a front door with multicolored abstract shapes painted into the inset panels, worms or vegetal tubes twirling into one another, a smeared seascape with yellow fingerprint stars. They entered the house to see the walls covered with framed paintings of the same style, clouds of paint with trails and coils and color, like fireworks across a green, smoky sky. Each was signed at the bottom: Eugene Andrew DeKeyser. Each painting had a small brass plaque. Each painting was named for Marie. And also along the walls were the photographs, black and white images of their daughter in costumes and headdresses, feathers and Christmas ornaments, holding scepters of chicken bone and tinfoil. In one she held a kitchen knife between her teeth, and a veil settled over her eyes. In many she was topless. Her parents were quiet.

"This is one I'm proud of," said Eugene, leading them to a photo on an easel on the dining room table. In it she was dressed as the Statue of Liberty, in a gauze wrap that left her entire body visible. "I did this one special for your visit. It's for America."

Marie entered the room. Her parents looked at her with her tiny waist, kohl eyes, and recently bobbed hair. She held out a plate of crackers and cheese and said: "Look Mom, Dad. My Eugene is an artist now."

"This is nothing but filth," said her mother. "You aren't covered in these pictures, Marie."

"An artist? I thought he was a baker," said her father. "There's money to be had there. Not in this mess that you've made of this house."

"Having a family is art. A child is art. Make a child," said her mother. "That's what you need to do."

"Only working four days a week, now? How can he take care of you?" said the father. "We can't stay here."

"We won't stay here," said the mother.

"You've made a mockery of this special day for America," said the father.

"You should be ashamed," said the mother. "Look at what you've done to celebrate freedom." She pointed to the photograph of her daughter as the Statue of Liberty.

They left the house, and found a place to stay for the night. Then they took a bus back to Munising. Marie told Eugene not to worry. She was reading a book. It said that real artists are never fully understood in their time. This only showed that he was, in fact, a real artist, she said. He was as real as could be. He had been shunned. That put him over the top, in her estimation. She knew he was good before. Now she knew he was great.

A day came when the two of them went out for breakfast, and Eugene sat reading the paper. This was months later. There before them were eggs and coffee and toast. Marie drank orange juice. She did not touch the coffee. Eugene was reading and thinking about the clay he had just purchased. He was making pots, now, becoming a potter. He made the pots and then covered them with leaves he formed from the clay. He drew spines and veins on each leaf with a little, sharp stick. He painted them green and let them bake in the sun. He read his paper and thought of leaves and Marie said she thought maybe she was pregnant and that they were going to have a baby.

And on the television, a plane had just flown into a tall building in New York City. They had not been watching the news or listening to the radio that morning. They were sitting, reading the paper, and had not noticed everyone gathered at the counter, looking at the television. But there it was. The diner was quiet, and no one was getting a warm up on coffee because the waitress was standing with the coffee pot held sort of loose in her right hand, and she was staring at the television.

"When did this happen?" asked Eugene.

"A couple of months ago, I think," said Marie.

"No," said Eugene, "this." He pointed to the television.

"Just this morning," said someone, maybe someone at the counter, maybe someone in a seat. Then Marie noticed, too.

Eugene and Marie went home after breakfast, and Eugene went to his studio to paint. He painted in oils on a wooden board. He mixed browns and greens in linseed oil, the heavy stinging scent curling his nose. He had four of Marie's brushes, each a different size. He spattered the board with paint in large, billowy clumps, and placed a big orange spot in the center. He used his nails to pull trails from the spot, scratching zigzags in them.

It wasn't long before people were talking about the Middle East. And talking about rogue nukes. And more. And he was going to have a baby.

At work he saw the bread loaves slowly rise and brown on top, and he thought about mushroom clouds slowly rising and plumping red and orange and brown. Walking home, he stopped at the high school's baseball diamond, and saw a confluence of breezes form a spinning dust devil. Cars suddenly started to backfire. Boy Scouts appeared around him in regiments. Birds fell unnaturally silent at no provocation that Eugene could perceive. The world began to spin a little faster, and Eugene began to feel it tumbling ever forward.

He brought his easels and paints upstairs, and found a corner for them in the dining room. He stuffed his clay beneath the sink. He went to the library and got a book on carpentry, and learned how to reinforce the supports in the basement. Marie played with the paints, and went to the beach to gather stones and shells, but Eugene never looked at them.

"I found these very long earrings," she said, "and I was thinking they would go good with that little Robin Hood hat. And I thought I could cut my hair very short, almost like a boy's."

"Not tonight, though," said Eugene. "I think I should figure out what to do about this basement door. I think I'll need to maybe replace it with something thick and made of metal. With some sort of round wheel that will seal it shut." Eugene spent the rest of the night looking at the door, thinking about the door, and wondering where he would get a wheel handle that would turn and seal the door. Marie went to the beach. It wasn't far along, but she was having a very pleasant pregnancy so far. She was not getting sick, and had been told that this meant she was having a girl.

She had heard this when she had started to meet the neighbor on the beach after not seeing her or speaking to her for what seemed like a long time. The neighbor, too, had rarely gotten sick, and she had had a girl. "Old wives tales are pretty accurate, huh?" she said to Marie. She explained to Marie all the wonderful and not-at-all wonderful things she could expect during her pregnancy and when she had her first child. "What does the artist think of all this?" she asked.

"The artist has a new project," said Marie.

"Two, really," said the neighbor.

"Or three," said Marie.

One weekend Eugene went out to the local dump and came back with sacks of broken mirrors. He used them to cover the outside of the house. "East side first," he said. "These will reflect light, and maybe some of the heat." In a month, he had only covered half the east side, but he had worked on other projects at the same time. He repainted the other walls of the house white. He tarred the roof so it was as black as it could be.

He tore out the picket fence, and pulverized the concrete statues. "We just can't afford to attract this much attention. We need to be less descript," he said.

"Our home is covered in mirrors," Marie said.

"Yes, but from a distance, they will reflect light, making the house invisible," Eugene said. He had read about that: about structures fitted with banks of light—this was pre-radar—that would blend into the ambient light, and make the structure disappear on the horizon.

He crated up his paintings, sure that they would burn easily, and be a danger to the house.

In her spare time, Marie learned how to make cookies and lemon bars, and started volunteering at the library. She learned how to shelve and how to shush people. Shushing would be a good skill to have when the baby was born, especially if she could master the sort of shush that sounded less tisky and more encouraging. She sat behind a counter as she got bigger, and stamped dates onto slips of paper glued into books. She felt herself expand, and she felt the baby kick. It kicked her right in the belly button one day, and she decided she would call her little girl Button. A real name, too, but Button would be her nickname.

Her mother and father told her Button was a very nice nickname for a baby, and also they told her to leave her pornographer husband.

Eugene started digging down. He broke open the concrete floor after he decided that the reinforcements wouldn't hold, and a metal door wouldn't sit on the hinges or seal correctly. He knew he needed a new level below their home. He had become very, very popular at the hardware store, and the manager always insisted on waiting on him. "This is what you really need," he'd say. "This will do the trick." And he sold Eugene a pick to break away rock and concrete, a wheelbarrow for the dirt, and a lamp on a long cord to see.

"Eugene," said Marie, "I think the baby is kicking."

Eugene muttered and continued to dig.

"Would you like to feel it?" she asked.

"I would like to make sure our home is terrorist-proof," said Eugene. "And then, once all this is done. Once all this very hard, very important work is done, yes. I would like to feel the baby kick."

At eight months, Eugene was looking for a place to store food, and Marie packed a bag and left.

On his roof, Eugene barely hears the phone ring. But it rings. On the roof, Eugene is laying down sod. He lays it over the shingles. He has a bucket of worms. He lays down the sod and sprinkles it with worms.

The sod will protect him. The roots of the grass and the dirt, the worms in their new home, the life force of organisms in cooperation. The birds that will be beckoned by the worms. The seeds carried in the guts of the birds and deposited on the dirt. Eugene has decided that the listening ears of the satellites of his enemies will be unable to penetrate the shield of life's energies. He will be hidden from the evildoers.

On the phone is Marie. Her child is eight months old and doing well. Her parents take care of the child when she is at work. She has had to get a job. He never answers the phone, and her parents have told her to stop calling.

"I can't," she says. "I want to talk to him."

She won't go back to the house. She won't bring the child with her.

The child is a boy and is named Raymond.

The sod and the worms and the birds will be a defense against ears in the distant sky that report to men in caves who wish to do Eugene harm. And Eugene's family, too. Soon the family will come home. He knows soon they will be back. How pregnant is she, now? The death rays will not harm us. The dirty bombs will be repelled by our shelter.

She calls every day. He ignores the phone, has forgotten what the ringing means.

stations

FOR MHLL

The Little Lamb could scream loud, but she seemed to love the radio. Uncle stayed in the car with her—she strapped into the car seat, he blowing cigarette smoke out the window. The Little Lamb drifted in and out. In and out. It was 2am.

The Little Lamb's daddy gave Uncle use of the car for the day, so Uncle could visit his ex and pick up his stuff. And so Uncle could head out to the big grocery store and stock up after a few weeks of walking over to the more expensive small market near his house. And so Uncle could drop in at an Escanaba bar and pay back the money he was fronted for a security deposit.

Terms of the car loan? Babysit the Little Lamb for one evening so her daddy and her mommy could have a night together. Uncle kicked away the dirty snow packed in the wheel well and it fell to the street. He drove hunched over to see through a hole in the fogged glass.

Daddy said: she likes the radio. If she doesn't sleep, try turning on the radio. Move around the dial, maybe.

The ex got the radio when she kicked Uncle out. Uncle got

to look for an apartment. So Uncle, unable to stop her in any other legitimate, non-baby shaking way, took the Little Lamb and strapped her into her car seat.

Uncle was, he was almost completely certain, not in a tailspin of any sort, even though he'd been made to believe so by the ex. He was just, he thought, on his way inside himself. It was a natural cycle in his moods. He was like dust on his eye, just at the edge of sight, always moving away from him as he followed it. It would get better, he had insisted. It did not do so in time.

The Little Lamb stirred. Uncle looked at her and tossed the cigarette butt out the window. He had smoked it to the filter. He had pulled it, a crooked, stubbed-out little thing, from the ashtray, seeing that it had at least three or four drags left, and he had stretched it out with his fingers, pulling it straight. He had lit the stubbed, black end, and brought it back to life.

It had cherry red lipstick on the end. The ex wasted more tobacco than she smoked. This was, he was sure, why he did not miss her in the slightest. She was given something in a limited supply, but was comfortable wasting it anyway.

Uncle found a station at the bottom of the dial. It was someone with a quiet voice, someone washed in static.

Do they think they are fooling us? Do they think we don't know? We can't examine evidence? Look things up? Did they think experts wouldn't ask questions? That we wouldn't ask question? Like, who benefited? Seriously, though: who benefited. Think about it.

Uncle thought about it. And for the life of him, he couldn't decide whom he thought benefited from any of it, really.

Like, was it better, the ex had wondered, to spend all one's time in the opposite end of the house, finding something that needed to be done there? Uncle thought sometimes.

The Little Lamb yawned and semi-opened her eyes. She semi-peered at Uncle.

Uncle said: you aren't fooling me, Little Lamb, Little Lamb. I see you looking at me under your lids. You can see me and I can see you.

The lids of the Little Lamb's eyes had delicate little blood vessels at the surface. That's the first thing Uncle had ever noticed about the Little Lamb. He shifted the dial ever so gently to see if the station would come in better.

This broadcast. Pirate radio, they'd call it. Free radio, I call it. They might be listening right now.

You hear about all that, even in the mainstream media. The taping of phone calls. The checking-up on things. You think they're looking for terrorists? Arabs? Muslims? Sleeper cells? They're looking for people like me. People who have discovered the truth. People who point up and say, the Emperor is not wearing any clothes. People who speak truth to power. People who watched those towers fall and know that buildings just don't fall like that. Fires don't melt steel like that.

I say it again: who benefited?

Uncle thought he recognized the voice. Like from someone he knew. Like a person he knew. Like this person he knew was on the radio. The signal sometimes went in and out. *I have see … than I will ever want to see. This is the world I … my children? This veiled world? This … lies?*

Uncle considered starting the car. Then he went ahead and started the car. He threw the second butt out the window, and sifted through the ashtray for another prospect.

Uncle thought north was the way to go first. It was the way to track the signal. Uncle thought it might be local.

I was talking to this guy. Real hard case. Real deep thinker.

Sitting at Main Street. Wouldn't listen to the evidence. Wouldn't approach me on my terms. Wouldn't even consider that he had been lied to. Just let it go. Just finish your beer, and have another, and let's all just let it go.

What the fuck about building seven, I said to him. What about that? Explain that.

He just turned back to the bar, turned away from me, and went back to his beer. Seriously. This was his reaction.

Main Street Tap. Up on third.

Uncle drove a residential block and noticed the signal getting stronger. The Little Lamb made a gurgle, or a burp, or possibly, she farted. There was a noise from the car seat, and Uncle wasn't paying close enough attention to tell what it was. He pulled over and looked at her. Fine. She was fine.

Uncle tracked the signal through the little town's grid of streets, each about big enough for two lanes of traffic, or one if when people parked after 7pm.

Such a town.

I should understand this. I should accept this. I should know that these are the people I am in contact with. These are my fellow Americans. These are the people who vote and pay taxes, who live and work, who drink and go hunting, who watch the Packers and raise their kids. Everything seems so easy to them.

And then I come along and shake their cages. I go right ahead and shake their God damned cages. Who benefited? What's happened since? Where's our country gone?

Why did 4000 Jews stay home on the 11th? Who called them and told them to stay home?

My cage has been shaken, people. My cage got good and shook up, and I'm sorry. I'm sorry, but I'm shaking yours, too. I am

*shaking the fucking cages. I'm coming up to your door, and I'm
knocking a little "Shave and a haircut, you're fucked."*

Uncle wished the man on the radio wasn't swearing, but
figured that the Little Lamb would forget the words long before
she started talking on her own.

Uncle drove around and around until the signal got very
strong. He stopped the car, and turned off the engine. And then
he turned the radio back on.

There was a house near him. A basement light was on. And
the house had a strange antenna. Uncle stared at it. His hands
itched on the wheel. His back felt funny against the wood bead
seat cover of his brother's wife. The weird, wood bead seat cover
that he counted imagine being at all useful for anyone in any
way.

*Building seven, building seven, building seven. I say it over and
over. He says it over and over. Yes, I say it over and over. Look into
it. That's what I'm asking. I repeat this stuff enough, and you'll
start to think, hey maybe there's something to it. Hey, maybe I
should do something besides, I don't know, be a fucking sheep?
Maybe I should check this out. Check out this building seven. Find
out about the cave-dwelling Arab scapegoat? Maybe I need to do
some research before I talk?*

*And maybe you'll just do that: maybe you'll just look it up so
that you can argue with me. I mean, that's all you ever do, right?
Maybe you'll go out there and try to find answers, so that I'll say
building seven, and you'll know what to say, right?*

*But when you look, you'll start to see. That's what's going to
happen. I guarantee it.*

Uncle looked at his watch. The Little Lamb's mommy and
daddy would be heading home soon. He could drive her back to

the house, and put her in her crib, and listen to her scream for half an hour and that would probably be okay.

He looked over at the house. The leaves had been raked and bagged. The bag was orange, and had the eyes and mouth of a Halloween pumpkin.

You're not listening. You're not listening.

I don't know why I do this, frankly. No one knows about it. No one's out there. This is just me. This is only me talking. This is me talking to me. Not to you.

But.

But maybe someone is there. Maybe someone hears. Maybe this will wake someone up.

The man was shouting. The man began to shout, and asking listeners to wake up. *Wake up! Wake up! Wake up!* he said.

Uncle started the car and blew the horn. He honked the beginning of Shave and A Haircut. *Honk honk honk honk honk.*

The radio went silent. Then the station went to static.

It woke up the Little Lamb. She cried in the backseat.

Oh, Little Lamb, said Uncle. Uncle's such a foolish, foolish man. I'm sorry Little Lamb. I'm sorry. Uncle was just playing with the man on the radio.

The Little Lamb cried all the way home, and for the next half hour straight through until Mommy and Daddy came home, and took her from Uncle's trembling arms. And in Mommy's arms, the Little Lamb began to quiet down again.

honey

I.

It's nice tonight. **Tonight?** Is it night? I don't think I know anymore.
I'm honestly unsure about the time. Or even just time. It's not
clear, here. We'll get to that later, though.

This is what happened when the index finger on the right
hand of a man from Iron Mountain, Michigan encountered, ever
so briefly, the point of a thorn on the stem of a rose purchased
at the Holiday Station store on Stephenson Avenue in the previ-
ously mentioned town of Iron Mountain, Michigan. (A full, in
bloom, red and very real rose, I mean. Not a little fake silk rose
in one of those glass tubes sold not for the rose but for the tube
to be used as a crack pipe. A real rose. A little wilted and brown
at its edges. But mostly fresh and open and deep red.)

A real rose and as such purchased for the purposes of
romance—as real roses tend to be. Imagine. Not illicit. Not
untoward. Not tragic.

Well, not really. A little tragic, maybe.

Because, to clarify, the rose was a rose purchased by a man smitten but not at that time enmeshed in the fibers of a relationship. An older man. I picture him in shirt sleeves and a knit tie. The ties four-in-hand knot—the most utilitarian of tie knots—loose and the top button of the shirt unbuttoned. A thin mustache. Ten hours growth on his neck and chin. A belt buckled through an added hole—a hole which may have been added for weight loss or for weight gain. I'm not sure which it's currently buckled in. When I picture the man I see him with holes added to both ends of the belt. And I'm not sure if this indicates that the man has had the belt for a long time, and needed, when younger and thinner to add an hole, or that the man is the sort of person who is big sometimes, and smaller other times. Who modulates the amount of space he wishes to take up in the world based on, say, his feelings of self-worth through any given year. Like: "This year, I deserve to fill more area," he thinks. "Hand over those potatoes."

An interesting side note, here: I imagine him saying things like that to no one—other than himself and, possibly, a pet reptile of some sort. A cold-blooded pet. One that sits in a tank, except when he, the pet—and, yes, I'm betting it's a male pet—is taken out to sit on a leg. The man's leg. When the man is watching, say, a Packer game. Which a man from Iron Mountain is, of course, wont to do. I can't imagine that this creature has a name. I mean, I know he does. I know that the man has named his pet lizard *something*. But I search and I search and I search my impressions of this man and I cannot find the name for the lizard with which he shares his life. I don't blame him for this, though. I blame myself. I blame my lack of compassion for him.

Compassion is harder and harder to claim these days. I find myself compelled to be as honest as I can with you. I'm sorry.

I'm sorry, one because I regret that you think less of me right now, knowing this about my waning compassion. I'm sorry, two, because—I'll just say it—you are on your way to where I am. And this likely is difficult for you to hear. You will sometime soon find it hard to access compassion as well. I say roll with it.

I was on the man, though. I should continue.

He's standing.

The man and his rose are standing over a record player. The plastic lid of the player is up, and it is resting against a window. It is dark out, and the man is using the window for a mirror. He sees himself in the glass reflected by the darkness of the night. He stands over the record player, and he holds the rose out to the mirror. And he speaks, but not to himself.

I mean, yes, really, he speaks to himself. He's looking at himself. He's the only one in the room. Here is my proof: if he was in the room with someone else, he would not be listening to Signals by the band Rush. Not that he's embarrassed. He is not, nor should he be, embarrassed to be listening to Rush. I only mean that Rush is nothing if not a solitary musical pleasure. Let's just put that out there. He'd have something else on if he had company.

He is and he is not speaking to himself. Because he is there in the image reflected through the window. But he has draped another person over himself. I mentioned that he is smitten. He is smitten with a girl. A girl who knows just a very little bit. That's also who he sees.

The girl is, by marriage, related to the man. By marriage. Let's not judge too harshly. Sister-in-law's sister? Is that even a thing? That can happen, right?

Many kinds of impropriety are here, I admit, lost to me as well. I don't think that's a thing. I think that's fine, isn't it? We're good?

I'm much more interested in the rose. He stands over the record player, the record spins beneath him, the speakers amplify the music to either side of him. He grasps the rose and his index finger—the soon to be ever-so-slightly injured finger—plucks the thorn. He has removed the green plastic phial with the water in it. A small drip of water from the bottom of the stem of the rose has fallen onto the end of his tie, but he can't see it in the window reflection, and I mention it here—needlessly, maybe? My attention shifts and focuses in ways I have trouble under-standing. But I believe that in the end, I need to honor this new way of being.

So I take back the word, "needlessly." Someone strike that.

He is giving a little speech, and he is watching himself, draped as he is with the aspect of this woman, to see how she will react. More precisely, though, he has split his consciousness to the best of his ability. One part of him is him speaking to her, and one part of him is her hearing him. He has been told that sometimes he gets a *maniacal* look in his eye when he talks to girls. Sometimes he betrays the gravity that weighs upon him when he confronts openly his feelings of admiration, of respect, of lust. So he is doing his very best to empty himself of that great weight. He pays himself attention. He watches his eyes and the micro-muscular movements of his areas around his eyes. He does not want to seem like a freak. Not again. Not with her. She is beautiful and she is calm and she called him *honey* once at a family gathering. And sometimes that goes so very far.

And she is in town again, tonight. Close by. And there is a party. And he is going to change and go to that party. And he is going to give the speech to the girl.

And without thinking it out, he presses his finger against the thorn on the rose, and it, with the familiar thoughtlessness of a thorn, breaks through the skin, pushes aside the muscle, and tears open a blood vessel. And draws free a drop of blood which tries to hold on to the surface of the finger, but because of a pained flinch, is separated and falls to the surface of Signals by Rush. Where it dries, nestled in the grooves of the song "The Weapon."

The man never plays this album again. The next morning he removes it from the turntable, puts it in its sleeve, files it under R in his Rush section. Further, he files it under S in the Rush section, because he prefers to file his albums by title instead of year of release. (We all have our systems.)

Some time after that—and I cannot with any certainty say when—the record is sold at a garage sale and it is driven south to the town of Gladstone, Michigan where it is given as a gift. To me.

I don't know what happened with him and the girl. And, really, I care less than you might imagine.

II.

More clearly than anything else from my life before, I remember this. I remember a haircut.

I sat on a folding chair on the back porch. I was under a rain poncho, under which was a ratty comforter—chewed through all over by a bored or frustrated or possibly fiber-craving cat. Michael's cat, Pizza. My older cousin's cat. And I shivered and I shivered.

It was 5 below 0. Colder with the wind. And there was wind. There was plenty of wind. It was cold, and from the last day's dusting of snow—too cold for a real, heavy, thick snow—the flakes were small and solid, and whipped around in little sparkling white funnels. I was with Michael, and he was cutting my hair.

He would not cut hair in the kitchen, even in the depths of winter: "I really, really don't want hair getting in my food," he'd say. He would not cut hair in the bathroom, even in the depths of winter: "I know you can sweep up, but you just can't get all the little strays, and I don't want to get hair stuck all over the bottom my feet after I shower. Willies, dude."

He would only cut hair on the porch, even in the depths of winter. So, heavy coats, comforter, poncho. And, for him, winter gloves. Heavy winter gloves and scissors with large handles to fit clumsy, gloved fingers.

He said: "The thing about a really good haircut is that a really good haircut is one that lasts much longer than a few weeks or a couple of months. It doesn't just look okay when you get it done. As it grows out, it still looks good—just in a different way. Like it was cut to grow out. That's what a good haircut does."

He said: "This is not a good haircut."

I replied: "That's okay. It just needs to hold out for a couple of weeks. Work complained." He cut. We talked.

He said: "You know that metal band, Celtic Frost? You know if you play a Celtic Frost CD after midnight, the devil comes? Or sends like a proxy demon to you? My brother played *Into the Pandemonium* by them once, and he said he watched the red power light on the stereo turn into an eye. And then it talked to him. About meditation."

I replied: "Your brother shoots Robitussin for dinner. Instead of eating food, he drinks Robitussin. Right from the bottle. All night."

He answered: "That just means he maybe has access to a part of the mind we all tend to usually turn off. That's all that means."

I said: "My grandfather has gotten to the point where now he no longer yells at the TV about the fact that he thinks there's a Communist in the White House. He doesn't even mention it to me when I visit him. And this has all happened in just the last couple of months."

He replied: "My dad's getting older. He doesn't walk as well."

I answered: "He sometimes gets this completely empty look in his eye and no televised Democrat can shake him from it. I go to visit and I just want him to yell 'pinko' at one of the Clintons so I know he's in there."

He said: "You know, the Nazis spent most of their real time and resources trying to conquer death. Not Europe. It's true. The inner circle was all occultists. Himmler. Goebbels. I read on the internet that Hitler said he wanted to grab God by his throat and shake him until his snap his neck. That the Nazis were planning to build this new Tower of Babel to attack Heaven eventually. That's why they were into rockets."

I replied: "I don't remember reading that. I just remember all the stuff about the war and the invasions and death camps."

He answered: "Yeah, that all sucked, too, apparently."

I said: "I guess currently I know only two couples on the verge of divorce, which has got to be some sort of record for lowest number of divorces among my friends and family. They both have kids this time, though. That's something."

He replied: "I used to get laid sometimes at weddings because of all the drinking. If they had some sort of divorce ceremony with an open bar, I'd be into twice as much trim."

I answered: "You usually use the word 'tail.' 'Trim' is a new one for you. Nice."

He said: "Did you ever see that Caligula movie the Hustler guy made? Where that old guy offs himself in that hot tub because he thinks there's a better world somewhere else. One without all the sodomy and murder or whatever. And, like, if he dies, he's not throwing his life away, but showing that he has hope for some other world."

I didn't reply. I just thought about how nice that sounded.

And wondered why it sounded nice. And I shivered a lot, too. It got colder and darker, and he sped through the last of the haircut, leaving some longer bits on the back of my neck.

When he was done, I gave him the two five dollar bills in my wallet. He let the wind sweep the porch. We carried his kitchen chair back inside and fit it beneath the kitchen table. On my way out, he told me to grab the bag near the door.

"That's for you. I found you a copy of *Signals* at this garage sale in Iron Mountain when me and Liz went up to visit her folks."

"Is it in good shape?"

"It was a dollar," he said. "I didn't check."

"Why were they selling it?"

"Who the hell asks 'why' at a garage sale, Chad?"

"K," I said.

"Maybe they listen to CDs like everybody else, Chad."

"K," I said. "I'm going to get going."

"Yes," he said. "Yes, you are."

"K," I said. "Later."

"Seriously," he said. "Leave."

And I did. And I went home. An okay haircut, my last one. Could've been worse. And I didn't need it long.

I went home and I put *Signals* on my turntable. I listened to it alone. Because, as I said before. Dot. Dot. Dot. I listened to "Subdivisions," and I listened to "The Analog Kid," and I listened to "Chemistry," and I listened to "Digital Man." And the song, "The Weapon," came on.

So, my parents were good people. And my heart was never majorly broken. And my grades in school were always just fine. And my day was livable. And my nights were a little lonely, but not all that bleak. And I wasn't losing my hair. And my weight was mostly under control. And I wasn't bullied. And I had a crappy job, but everybody has a crappy job.

It's just that everywhere around me, everything kept moving. And I couldn't do anything to stop that. I'd accepted that I couldn't do anything to stop it. I just didn't really *like* anymore that I couldn't do anything to stop it. I imagined if I was somehow a bigger individual, maybe I'd have more control over the continuing move forward of everything. If only I was bigger.

Then a line came on in the song. "He's not afraid of your judgment/He knows of horrors worse than your Hell/He's a little but afraid of dying/But he's more afraid of..." And then the record skipped back to "...horrors worse than your Hell."

So that's it. That's when I met the man I spoke of earlier. He was dried there in the grooves of the record. I took it off the turntable and felt it with my fingertips, and felt a spot that flaked. I grabbed a paper towel and put a little water on it. I rubbed the spot, and it came up rust red. When the water melted the dried substance, it smelled a little like blood. And then a lot like blood when I held it to my nose. It was the man crossing my path and giving me a message. Conspiring with everything else to give me a message. "...A little bit afraid of dying." Only a little.

I smelled the blood and I smiled and I knew him and I used my belt to hang myself in my closet. And I hung there just filled with hope.

III.

I swear I hear music. Not hear, though. That's imprecise. *Know* music. Around me.

In this here, now, whenever place, I have learned some things about the universe. I have learned that the universe, vast and general and all-encompassing as it is, desires something unexpected from us. I've learned that the universe desires, of all things, specificity from us. The universe does not do well with ambiguity. It wants us to know what we want and to want what we want. When I died, I had a great deal of ambition. A great, unformed cloud of ambition and desire, expanding and growing and doubling and quadrupling with every second of my last conscious thoughts in my last body.

It's like a head rush, by the way. Death. Maybe so because of the means of my self-ending. But crawling fingers of blackness conquering my vision, and this throbbing elation as the blood stopped flowing. And all this hope in me, tossing every other thought and feeling free from my brain. They call murder by tossing someone from a window defenestration. Hope defenestrated every other state of being within me—good ones and bad. Positive and negative.

I know so many new words now, by the way. I have access to so much more. And so much less.

So there I was hoping for big and significant, and there I was blinking out and sort of exploding. And the pieces turning and changing. And then here.

No eyes. No ears. Memories, though. Which is nice. And something in contact with something else.

This feeling of great size. This *body* that seems to have grown in circles and larger circles and larger circles. This body that is in contact with cold and with damp. And is cold and is damp. Lots and lots of *me*. And this continuity of consciousness throughout me.

I spent an hour or a day or a year or 16 years screaming. Waiting for someone to hear the scream. Just screaming. After the first few minutes or hours or months or four years, I even gave up on words. I just put out a sound. Or tried to put out a sound. I had much of the same mind that I had started with, so I knew the meaning of sound. And the control of the neurological mechanisms for creating sound. I just didn't have the physical apparatus anymore. So eventually I stopped. Then I spent either twice the time I had spent screaming or half the time I had spent screaming *running*. That was equally unsatisfying. When you are not a mobile creature, but you were a mobile creature, and you remember what it was like to be a mobile creature, wanting to move and not having anything *to* move is the greatest torture.

But only for a couple of decades. Or centuries, maybe.

Eventually a man introduced me to what I am. The previous occupant. I caught a quick glimpse of him, heard a quick echo. He had left a sort of graffiti on the wall of the body, and as the body expanded it broke down, became "unreadable." Once I had finished with the screaming and the running, I noticed the last of it, of what may have been a very long correspondence— perhaps quite an enlightening one. Instead, I was left with a line or two:

"Hello, you. Welcome. I have had other jobs—I like to write music, for example—but I consider myself, mostly, a mushroom identifier. Imagine my joy, then, in being able to identify myself as such." I'm not sure if the previous occupant vacated willingly or if I pushed him out. After I found that note (one of his first? One of his last?), I found no more. Our moments together were brief. Or decades long. I honestly don't think I know the difference. They *felt* brief. And then his message disappeared.

Not far from where I lived is Crystal Falls, Michigan. My father fills the car with gas. My mother packs a lunch. My family drives an hour and forty minutes—my brother and I separated by the cooler so we don't complain about our car seat property rights. We drive and drive and find ourselves in Crystal Falls, Michigan. And then we drive and drive south to the forest nearby in Mastodon. And then we picnic with the Humungous Fungus—acres and acres, tons and tons of a single mushroom. A colony mushroom beneath the earth. The largest in the world. The biggest thing I have ever known about. Now me.

I say this again: The universe requires specificity, and we should give specificity to the universe because the universe is lazy, and too literal, and will drop you very close to home if you don't offer it a better idea. If you are reading this, you are in the same place I am, and I don't give you this advice for this life, but for the next. My goals are generally the same for the next time through, but they have been, let me assure you, thoroughly hashed out. Believe you me. And do as I have done. Hash out the future.

And I don't know if I left this place willingly—and I don't even know if such a thing is possible but I am looking into it—or if you pushed me out to take my place. I may not be able to know, but I offer thanks to you, anyway just in case. Really. Thank you very much.

anymore

Anymore, it's not so much done as talked about. Time was the lot of us thought of it as a point of pride, or a very worthwhile entertainment, this sticking it to them we did.

There was Charlie, six-foot-nothing in his boots, black hair in lazy reeds over his eyes. There was Enit in a blue raincoat, Enit with the paint spattered pants, and clove scented sleeves. There was Riley; two times the man of any of us. And there was me, Billy Job, brought up as well as could be expected, brought up as quietly as possible, brought up in a shiny white room with a comfortable bed and clean pillowcases.

Solid group, top to bottom. And there was a top. And there was certainly a bottom. Me. Billy Job was always on the bottom.

And when it wasn't nothing but talking for too long, I pushed buttons. Charlie's buttons, the biggest in the group. Believe you me, easy to push. I told him we never do anything but talk and drink those beers you bring. Riley said what's wrong with the beers and why don't you shut it, Billy Job.

That Charlie, he was quiet. Blue Enit, he asked what we should do, and Charlie sipped his beer, and slurped at the excess from the ditch that circled the top of the can—you know how it collects up there and then he asked what the hell Billy Job thought we should do.

I said tonight we should go out and break every damn window on Third Street. And Charlie, top dog, he decided that was a pretty good idea.

So, that's what we did. 3 AM, we met at one end of Third, passed out the baseball bats and hammers, and went to work.

And, anymore, when I think of what it is Heaven must be like, I think about that hour on Third Street, where the glass shattered and fell like snow, and caught the light, glittery.

I think of Enit's pirate cackle, and the spray of glass from the end of his hammer.

I think of Riley skipping from the hardware store to the Gypsy Bar, uncontained.

I think of Charlie, patting my back, filling my ear with all kinds of praise.

I think about the glass crunching under my boot, again like a snow new-fallen, unsullied.

And no one got caught, and the police never showed, and that was just right.

And anymore, it's talk talk talk.

daredevils

I thought I would find Swenson on the trails and drive a nail into his hand. He had called my little brother a very bad name, and as he was getting off the bus he hit him on the top of the head with the flat of his right hand. My brother, Lee started crying but I didn't have time to react before Swenson got off the bus. Swenson had his smirk—we could see him through the bus window just smirking, and then waved up at us as we drove by. I wanted to get off and follow him, but the bus driver wouldn't let us because it wasn't our stop. "I can't legally," she said. "I can't legally let you off my bus unless you are at your official, designated spot. I could get sued. Sued in court."

I had a long nail I'd found when Lee and I went to the construction site where they're building the house next to us. I thought we should get Swenson alone, gang up on him, hold him down, and drive the nail into his right hand, so that when it ached, he'd remember that it was the hand he used to hit my brother.

°

Nights earlier, we're all sitting together at the dinner table, pawing and grabbing at the food in front of us when my oldest brother Gary elbowed Lee so hard, Lee spit milk into his own lap. Of us four kids, none had waited for the prayer, and Dad had the look on his face. Gary was the first to notice the look, so he was the one who gave an elbow to Lee, second youngest. The elbow settled rough into the divot of Lee's armpit—Lee reaching over the table for another fish stick—and my little brother let out this wheeze/grunt combo noise. It got everyone's attention, and then we saw Gary seeing Dad, and the look on Dad's face. The disappointed look. Dad, brow furrowed under his balding head; flat, rigid nose pointing straight out at Gary; tiny brown eyes tinier and tinier.

When we saw Gary, and saw that he was looking over at Dad, we knew Dad was waiting for the prayer.

Mom, she just stood in the doorway between the dining room and the kitchen, her boyfriend's arm around her waist. I'm pretty sure she rolled her eyes. I'm pretty sure he rolled his eyes first.

It wasn't every night we had dinner with Dad. He was only over at Mom's boyfriend's house with us every other Saturday. Because of that, the kids—the three boys, the girl—were prone to forget that before we ate with Dad, there was always the prayer. Dad's expectation—that his kids would, when they found themselves fortunate enough to have another meal provided for them, that when they sat down at a table and prepared to eat, they would offer a prayer to God for allowing there to be another meal. It was an expectation of his that this was something we would always do, whether he was there or not; for the rest of our lives, we would offer the prayer and count ourselves lucky.

Gary bowed his head first and had the best memory for the

routine. Lee followed, and then around the table it went, from Lee to me. From me to Katie. When it made the circuit, Dad bowed his head. He spoke clear and we followed if we could. Lee and Katie, the two youngest, eleven and five, couldn't. "Lord Jesus Christ, friend of sinners, we thank you for friendship, prince of peace, we ask you that we may be peacemakers. Lord of all, we thank you for this food. Bless it to our bodies, we pray. Amen."

"Amen," we said.

After dinner, Lee and I went to the hill in the backyard, where we'd dug up a track for our Hot Wheels cars. Some of it was the orange plastic track I got for my birthday. Some of it was dirt—we'd ripped up the grass at the root, pulled out little stones. We'd dug a hole, too, and Lee grabbed the hose and filled it with water. The hole opened at the end, and the opening was covered with a piece of beaverboard we took from the construction site next to the house. I pushed a car around on the dirt track, up to the top of the hill.

"Blow the dam when I give the old say so," I said. Lee said okay, and I put the car on the track. "Ready?" I said.

Lee said yeah.

"Now!" I said, letting go of the car. It rolled down the track, and Lee pulled the board away, making a *kaboosh* noise with his mouth. The water poured out the hole, as the car skittered down the track. A stream of the water crossed the track, but the car beat it by a few seconds. "Evel Knievel does it again!" I said to the television audience. Lee whooped.

"Refill the dam," I said. "Let's try it again, but this time, we'll blow it earlier."

Lee said yeah in that way he does.

"Can Evel Knievel survive?" I said to my television audience.

They thought probably.

"Someday," I said to Lee, "it'll be us in the car."

Lee scratched at the dry skin on his ankle, and said okay. In that way he does that, too.

Mom had sat down with me when the breakup happened. She said it was very important that I never, ever cry, and I never, ever have. She and I got a shoebox from the basement, and we cut a slot in the top. In the slot, I was supposed to put notes. She said it was like at work, when someone puts up an employee comment box. I was supposed to make comments, and she would read them. And if there was something important in them, she would have a meeting with me about it later.

A couple of days after she put the box up, and told the other kids about it, too, mom's boyfriend—who had sort of moved in to make sure Dad didn't come around while Mom got her stuff packed and we could move—took it down.

Eventually, we went to Mom's boyfriend's house to live, and Dad was allowed to visit after he proved that he could do it without causing a fuss.

Mom's boyfriend came out into his backyard, and when he saw what Lee and I had done to the lawn, he kind of freaked.

He said some words Dad would never say.

He was mad because we had dug the hole on the side of his hill, and we pulled up some of his grass to make a dirt trail up to the orange track. He asked whose idea it was, and Lee says it was his—even though we both sort of came up with it. Then Mom's boyfriend smacked Lee.

Dad heard the commotion, and all the swearing. He came out to see what was going on. He told Mom's boyfriend to not ever take the Lord's name in vain around his kids, but Mom's boyfriend didn't hear it because he was too busy yelling at Lee.

When Mom's boyfriend hauled off and hit Lee in the mouth, Dad came up behind him and gave him a shove. Mom's boyfriend stumbled forward, and he fell on top of Lee, who was crying from the smack. Mom's boyfriend got up, and Dad was standing over him.

Dad's taller than Mom's boyfriend, but he doesn't work out or anything like that. Mom's boyfriend has big arms, and the way he talks, you can tell he gets into fights all the time when he goes out to bars. He wears a t-shirt, and his arms fill out the sleeves, and sort of stretch them. His legs aren't as strong, but they're still pretty large in his cutoff denim shorts.

Dad had on the polo shirt, the blue one with a little alligator. His arms don't fill out the sleeves at all. But, anyway, Dad didn't back down when Mom's boyfriend stood up and got in his face. And he didn't really flinch when Mom's boyfriend fake punched at him. He just stood there and said that he didn't want the guy ever to say the Lord's name in vain around his kids. It's important to him, he said. "You know I love you," he said. "You take good care of my kids and my wife. I just want you to do that one thing for me."

When Mom's boyfriend laughed and went over to the picnic table to grab a can of beer he left there, Dad walked to Lee and asked him about digging up the grass on the lawn. Lee said he did it, and I told Dad that I helped do it, too. Dad looked at me and thanked me for being honest.

Then he smacked me. He said we should both be punished equally for what we did, since we were both responsible. My eyes stung a little and I told him yes, he's right, it's only fair, when he asked if I agreed with him. Dad made us both go over and apologize to Mom's boyfriend for what we did. Dad told us he was going to give our allowance directly to Mom's boyfriend for the next couple of months, and that we were going to have to do all the yard work that we were told to do, and be like Mom's boyfriend's slaves until he said we were done.

About a week into living with Mom's boyfriend, I got up to get some water after going to bed. Mom's boyfriend's house smells weird, like some kind of dry cheese. I was walking around with my water, and smelling to see if I could track down the source of the odor, but it was everywhere. It was just the way the entire house smelled.

I walked by the TV room, and heard Mom talking to her boyfriend. She was laughing and slurring her words, and so was he. "I guess I am kind of a slut, Clint," she said. Then they both laughed more.

Our little sister Katie tried to follow Lee and me when we went out to ride bikes, but she was slow and on training wheels, so we managed to get away from her quick. She yelled as she pushed her pedals with her feet, and her sandals kept slipping off, and she shouted how Mom said we had to take her with, we had to take her with.

We cut through our neighbor's yard and slipped onto one of the trails that circle and crisscross the neighborhood—The Bluffs—where we lived. We were riding over to our friend Kevin's house, where we were going to pick him up, and have him come out and ride bikes, too. We were going to look for Swenson, who lived on the opposite side of The Bluffs, and was usually out riding the trails in the evening, just like us.

Lee had a forearm-long piece of rebar in his backpack. I had a long stick—a half a piece of axe handle—that my older brother Gary sanded and covered half in black duct tape as a grip. He drilled a hole in the end and tied a leather strap through it, so I had it hanging from my wrist, and it swung as we rode. It banged into my knee when we hit bumps.

We rode around and around, but didn't run into Swenson until late, in gray, gray evening. And when we did, he was with a couple of older boys who we thought were probably his brothers. We'd never met them. They were waiting on one of the trails, the three of them in a line blocking it so we couldn't get by. One of the older boys had acne and a hooded sweatshirt with Escanaba Wrestling written on it in white letters. He asked us what we were doing, and Swenson shifted back and forth in his seat with that same smirk from earlier when he hit Lee.

"We're just riding around," I told him. He said it looks to him like we're out trying to find trouble of some kind or another. The other older boy said it looked like that to him, too, what with me carrying the nigger knocker and all.

Lee whistled when the boy said the n-word. Dad had told him not to say that word anymore, even though Mom's boyfriend said it, and some of his Special Ed classmates said it.

The boy in the sweatshirt told him to shut up and asked what I had the club for.

I said: "I'm just carrying it. I'm bringing it home."

The other older boy was in a black, sleeveless Metallica t-shirt, and had a collection of a dozen or so long stray hairs on his chin. He was grabbing them and pulling, twisting. He told me to let him see it and I said no. He said it again, saying give it fag, but I still didn't offer him the bat, so he got off his bike and walked over to me. He said, seriously you little shit, let me see the nigger knocker. He grabbed at it with one hand and used the other to steady my bike. We each pulled, and he was stronger than me, but my wrist got caught on the leather strap. He got very close and he smelled like cigarettes. It took him some time to twist it from my fingers. "Cut it out," I said.

He started to twist it, and the strap tightened around my wrist. It got tighter and tighter, and he kept pulling until I was pressed up against the handlebars and my hand turned purple.

I wanted him to take it from me, but he'd twisted it so much it wouldn't come off. My bike was slipping under me, and pulling me down while he pulled me forward. Lee shouted for him to stop. I was too focused on my wrist to notice what anyone else was doing, I just heard Lee's yelling, and felt tingles in my hand. I was on one leg when my bike toppled to the side. That pulled me down, all but my hanging wrist. I tried to think about how I could twist myself out, and pull off an escape. But I couldn't move and it hurt too much to think.

The older boy in the Metallica t-shirt let go, and my arm fell. And then my body fell completely. The handlebars jammed into my groin, and I started to feel sick from the pain. Metallica t-shirt reached down and unspun the strap, and pulled the club from my hand.

He took the club, and he hit a tree with it. It didn't do much— just dented the bark—so he hit it again. And then again. He hit until one of he pulled a blow, and the end snapped off some of the bark. Cool, he said, and I'm keeping this, he said. Lee said something like you can't because our brother made it. Swenson and the boys rode off down the trail as I was getting up. I tried sit on my bike, but my groin still stung from hitting the handle-bars, so I walked the bike out to the road, and walked all the way back home.

Lee followed, riding slowly, and in big circles around me. Kevin went the opposite way, riding back home. I wasn't crying, because what had happened didn't make me want to cry. Before Lee and I went in our Mom's boyfriend's house, I said, "I don't think we should ever go back to school again," and he agreed. So, we decided that the next day, and forever after, we were going to skip school.

Gary didn't notice the missing club for a few more days. By then, we all have a lot more to think about.

°

Mom liked to buy books and videos about stunt drivers for Lee and me. She bought us red, white, and blue paints for gray, plastic car models, and helped us draw stars on them. She could always make the lines of the stars a lot straighter than we could. She bought Matchbox cars. We were going to drive fast someday. Very fast. One day you would find us in a car, throwing ourselves into the air.

We even went to a monster truck rally once. But we had to leave when the noise started to hurt Lee's ears.

The morning after, with my wrist still sore, we left like we were going to meet the bus, but we didn't. At the end of the block we went right instead of left. And into the trees. And past the trees to a trail we knew, and from the trail we went all the way to the railroad tracks. It was Lee and me. Just us.

At the tracks, we began to walk south. Around the tracks, there were piles of pig iron pellets. I grabbed one and rolled it around in my hand. We walked, heading out to the junkyard behind the paper mill.

There was an empty construction site. Lee and I walked into the house, just a blond wood frame at that point. It would be two floors, but the stairs weren't in yet. The north wall was finished, but the rest was skeletal. It smelled like fresh cut wood. We hung from beams. We kicked over a sawhorse. Lee found a long nail and brought it to me.

He told me to look, look, and I stopped throwing rocks at the finished wall and looked. Lee handed the nail to me.

"This is nice," I said, holding the long, silver nail. "Looks deadly."

Lee smiled and tried to grab it back. "No," I said. "You might get hurt. I'll hold it."

Lee frowned and said he wouldn't in that way of his.

"You know what we're going to do with this?" I said. "We're going to drive this into Swenson's hand. We're going to pierce right through his palm. We're going to nail him to something with this. You and me."

Lee agreed.

At night, the paper mill gave off a cloud of this rotten egg smell, but not during the day. All day we walked and talked. We decided that definitely when we saw Swenson alone on the trails, we were going to nail him up—as long as the older boys weren't with him. We talked about how Swenson looked like some jerky little sitcom actor, the way his hair is blond and parted on the side. And the collared shirts, the short-sleeved collared shirts he wore every day. They were never wrinkled. On picture day, he wore a tie. He lived on the side of The Bluffs with the nice houses, the bigger houses with all the other rich people. He told everyone all the time how much his dad made, and everyone just had listened because their dad didn't make as much.

"It's not a contest," I told him once, but he said I only said that because my family was poor and my mom and dad were divorced. His family is Catholic, he said, and he told me my parents' divorce was, like, the biggest sin possible, except for the sin of being queer bait. Which made me a sinner who was also the product of sin, he said.

This one time, Dad and Gary were fighting. Dad asked Gary why none of us ever told him about Mom's boyfriend. "You all knew about it. Why didn't you say anything?"

"We all like Mom better, Dad," he said. He apologized later.

Lee told me he got on the bus and the older girl in front of him turned around and asked if he was a Taylor brother. "You're a Taylor brother, aren't you?" she asked. He nodded, and she got a look on her face like she wanted to pull his ear off with her teeth and spit it back at him. She turned, and mentioned my name to the girl next to her, and they laughed.

Lee had a chin like mine, with a little dent in it. He had a cowlick in the back of his head, around this whorl of hair. He sat in the bathroom before school combing it. He held the comb under the faucet and combed at the spot, trying to get the hair smooth against his head. A lock always remains pulled away, no matter how short or long his hair was. He couldn't make it stick to his head, though he combed and combed. I used to have to do the same thing until I decided not to care anymore. After that, I gave Lee the can of foaming hair gel my mom bought for me. It never worked either, and I tried to tell Lee that. He didn't listen. He kept combing. He got on the bus some mornings with a white dab of foam on his ear, or on the collar of his shirt. I tried to check before we get on, because I didn't want anyone to notice and say something to him. Sometimes, I missed.

I gave Lee my round, mirrored sunglasses. He wore them until the legs broke off the hinges, and then Mom helped him to take a piece of stretchy thread, and tied them to his head.

Behind the paper mill, we found the junkyard. It was full of all the things the paper mill had gotten rid of, like broken swivel chairs and old computers. We found a keyboard in perfect shape, and put it in my bag. I said I thought I might be able to build myself a computer if I found a book at the Carnegie library, and came back out to find the parts. It would take me a while, but I had plenty of time.

I said that that made me the mechanic. If we were daredevils, me and Lee, I'd be the one who fixed up the cars and made sure the tricks worked by knowing math and angles. I'd know the speed we needed to get to if we were going to jump a line of cars.

And then I said Lee'd be the driver. He'd be the one who knew how to take the turns just right, how to fishtail, and ride on two wheels to get us through tight spots.

I'd sometimes flick a cigarette out the window, and it would hit a line of gas, and the flame would follow it to a car. The car would blow up.

I told Lee that he could also be the one who sits inside the little barrel covered in dynamite. Someone would light the wicks on the barrel, and after a few seconds, all the dynamite would explode. I told Lee he'd even have on a straight jacket, and be handcuffed to the bottom of the barrel, so everyone would know that he couldn't get out. But he wouldn't need to. I told Lee that all the dynamite would explode at the same time, and all the explosions would cancel each other out, and he'd be fine. And while the wicks were burning, he'd even get himself out of the strait jackets and the handcuffs.

We walked for a long time, at least until dusk. Then Lee and I headed home. As we walked, I put my arm around him, and we walked crossing our feet in front of each other like the Monkees did at the beginning of their TV show.

We didn't hear Swenson ride up until he was very close. We had to jump to get out of his way, and Lee landed in a sticker bush. Swenson road by, and skidded out, kicking dirt and turning to us. He laughed. "What are you, boyfriends?" Swenson said. "You were holding him and walking like he's your boyfriend, Denny."

"Shut up, Swenson. Fuck the hell off," I said.

"You two are boyfriends. Fucking faggots," Swenson said.

Lee was getting up, and I was getting up. Swenson was laughing. He stopped, though, when Lee hit him with a rock. He fell over on his bike. Lee started running at him, and I followed.

"Get him!" Lee said.

Swenson was tangled and couldn't get up. Lee arrived first, and dropped on top of him. I came after. Lee sat on his chest, and pinned Swenson's arms down with his knees. "Hold him down," I said. "Hold him right there," I said.

Swenson was next to a tree stump. His arm was right up against it. I pulled his arm, and laid it flat on top of the stump. The stump had been cut with a chain saw, probably. I had him by the wrist, and his palm was open in the center of the tree stump. I tried to put the hand so that the center of his palm was over the middle dot, inside of the rings. I did that with my left hand, and with my right I reached into my backpack. I rummaged around until I found the long nail at the bottom, below my books, below my pencil case. I held the nail in my hand point down. "Hold him still," I said to Lee.

"Get fucking off me. Get fucking off me," Swenson said. He struggled. "Get fucking off me."

"This is for you," I said.

I put the point of the nail into his palm, and I started to press. I started slow. I didn't know how much pressure it would take to drive the nail into his hand and through to the tree stump. I didn't know how strong I had to be to push the nail all the way into the tree stump, so far through that he would have to work the nail back and forth to dislodge it, so he could go home and bandage his hand.

I didn't know if I was strong enough, but I pressed. Swenson yelled, and I pressed. He started to cry, and I pressed.

Dad came over for dinner on the weekends, but we never went over to his house. It was small. Too small. Too small for three brothers and a sister. Too small for the Taylor brood, which is what Dad called us. "Well, I'd love to have the whole Taylor brood over, but you're just too many. Your mom and I probably should've been less enthusiastic about making you."

So Dad came over to Mom's boyfriend's house every other weekend. He brought stuff for us. Gary liked music, so Dad brought him tapes by bands he thought were appropriate. Lee liked baseball, so Dad brought him a packet of baseball cards. Katie liked pretty much anything stuffed, so she got a stuffed animal. Dad brought me Christian comic books, because he thought the one's I usually bought were too violent and Godless.

Mom always inspected the gifts after Dad left. She'd smirk, or she'd roll her eyes, or she say, "Well, this isn't so bad, I guess." If the gifts were disappointing, then she'd take us to ShopKo and we'd look for something, and—if it wasn't too expensive—we'd get a "make-up gift."

When a little trickle of blood sprung from the point of the nail, I jumped back. It was only a drop. It was only a very small dot of blood in the wrinkly surface of his hand. But I jumped back and dropped the nail. When I pushed myself back and fell on my butt, Lee looked at me. Lee looked at Swenson's hand. It was starting to really bleed. Swenson thrashed, and Lee fell to the side. Swenson got up. He stared at his hand, blood water-falling from the heel of his hand onto the ground, and then he started to moan. He grabbed his bike. His blood smeared on the handgrip. He got on the bike and pumped his feet, and went away down the trail, fast. Lee and I were still on the ground. We hadn't moved. We listened to Swenson yelling as he rode home. He didn't scream words. We didn't hear words. We just heard a scream.

Lee started to laugh, and kept laughing all the way home. We took our time getting home, and when we got there, a police car was waiting in the driveway, and Mom was waiting in the driveway, and so was Mom's boyfriend. Mom's boyfriend was talking to a cop, and he was pointing this way and that.

Me, I thought about flicking a cigarette and blowing up the nearest cop car. Lee wasn't afraid of the handcuffs at all, and held his arms out in front of him when the officer.

grown in

Give it a good, long, hard look and you will see: nothing becomes me quite like nothing does. I am—motherfucker—the Howling Wolf of Escanaba, Michigan, you might say. I am the last living man who really remembers what it means to be Northtown. I am the soul and the splendor—motherfucker—of all that is thrown in your face whenever you make it over to my side of town.

And speaking of faces, I've been growing into mine for a long, long time. But it's all inflated and pushed up to the edges now. Really, so what's left to say?

Northtown exhales fire from its terminal blocks at the cars that stray too close. Northtown lets cops visit, but only for short—and we never let them descend into the interior alleys and nuclear blocks where the real work of living goes on. Be mine. Be my little baby. Go buy me some mothballs and score me some pills from the drugstore up the street. The one where they still don't check ID. And when you come back? Then we'll talk.

Then we'll talk.

Take it outside, and take that one—that little one, the drape chewer there—take the little one with.

My baby, she says, "Lord, love my baby with the cauliflower ear." She says it.

Anymore, there's nothing else to say. So take a good, hard look. Look at what's grown.

rabbit fur coat

Boy had black duct tape wrapped in rings around the little purple warts on his fingers. Someone had told him after a couple of weeks like that, the warts would fade away. It had been a couple of weeks, but so far, no dice.

"What's that? So you remember you're a fag?" a Lundberg said. One of the taller ones. He was standing behind Boy, hands in pockets, in a small crowd, half Lundbergs, half others.

Boy ignored them, closed the metal door and spun the tumbler on his locker two times, then three more. He curled his books up in his arms, turned away, and a punch landed on the back of his neck, bending him, and throwing him, and tumbling him forward. He smacked against the wall. The Lundberg brother responsible laughed. And then the others laughed.

Sarah sat in front of him in fifth period study hall. He came in late, cleaned up as he could get. A bloody hunk of tissue stuck from his nose, red at the nostril. She mouthed what happened. Lundberg, he mouthed back.

They talked about it at lunch.

"Whatever happened to tripping? Or yanking books?" he said, pulling at the tissue and examining at the dried red spots.

"In my day," she said, "bullies didn't hurt you so much as humiliate you with scathing comments on your hygiene and personal style."

"The good old days," said Boy.

"Here's to them," said Sarah, raising a can of Coke, half-filled with whiskey from her father's liquor cabinet. They tapped cans and tipped them back. They drank and crushed the empties.

She gave him a tape she'd made for him, a collection of songs from some new records. One side was Echo and the Bunnymen, Bauhaus, Joy Division. The other was an album called Meat is Murder by The Smiths. "Who are The Smiths?"

"You'll like them," she said. "Gloomy. Made for you."

In study hall, Boy rolled and rolled and rolled a twelve-sided die. It was his favorite of the polyhedrals—his role-playing dice. He kept them in the pocket of his backpack. Six-sided dice he stole from family board game boxes. The others procured from a game shop in Marquette. The pyramid-shaped four sided dice. The two ten sideds like little tops, thrown together to roll percentages. Eights. Twenties. All light blue plastic, and sold with a white crayon to fill the numbers. But, the twelve, was best, all interlocked pentagrams and rarely used.

Maybe it was the number 12. A better age than his current one. The age when he woke up to find a small stain on his sheets that meant he had reached puberty. Twelve months in a year and twelve donuts in the boxes at the tables after the service at church his grandparents took him to. Twelve apostles for the fake Son of God. Base-twelve and a "School House Rock" cartoon with a twelve-toed boy.

He liked that especially. Bad at math, usually, Boy still liked the idea. If people were born with twelve fingers and toes instead of ten, everyone would multiply by twelve as naturally as they multiplied by ten now. A quirk of nature, a fluke of birth could change so much. An extra finger or an extra toe, and people wouldn't measure their lives in decades. They would gather their lives in dozens.

He thought with time he could train himself to think in base-twelve. His friend Hockey thought he couldn't, that no one could. Hockey was a hack-and-slash psychopath when they played. He never thought things through. So Boy didn't listen to him.

After school, Hockey drove them home, singing along to his WASP tape. Boy knew Hockey well enough to know he'd never fucked, much less like a beast, but Hockey screeched the chorus to "Fuck Like A Beast" along with Blackie Lawless, anyway. A train blocked the entrance to the interstate south, and stuck Hockey's beater behind a school bus. Behind his razor sunglasses, he stewed. His hair draped his neck, frosted blond and spiky on the top. "Just like Brian Bosworth," he said. Kids in the back of the bus, middle-schoolers, stuck out tongues, and Hockey flew the bird their way.

"Fuck you," he said, sticking his head out the window. A chorus of single finger salutes rose from the bus's back row.

Boy laughed, and smoked one of Hockey's cigarettes, even though they were Marlboros. "Camels are better," he said. He had chewing gum to mask the smell on his breath for when he got home.

"You got your one-hitter? Wanna get high?" Hockey asked.

"Nothing in it. Town's dry," Boy said.

Hockey spit brown into a dented Mountain Dew can, reached over, and punched Boy's shoulder. "This town is never dry. No town is ever dry."

"Fucker," Boy said.

"My car, I get to punch you," Hockey said. "Your car, you can punch me."

"Yeah, car," said Boy. "My car. When I get one. If I get one."

"Maybe from your grandparents?"

"Not likely." Boy smoked with the cigarette inverted, palmed. The smoke trickled out from under his pinky, and dribbled out through his nose.

Back home Boy went to the bathroom. Younger, he played a game where he had to leave the bathroom before the refilling of the toilet ended, imagining it as the countdown to an explosion. Older, he didn't mind, but sometimes saw himself blown through the wall; ripped apart by hot, swift gusts of fiery air; scattered; his fingers embedded in the plaster; the bones of his toes like nails into the floor; his teeth, shrapnel. Now he rubbed his eyes. His grandmother knocked on the door to call him to the dinner table.

That night, Boy thought about the game on Saturday. Hockey was going to show up in the afternoon to role-play until late into the night. (He was the only one left who still played. All the other boys had peeled away from the group toward girls and parties.) Hockey usually brought vodka in a flask, or they stole it from Boy's grandpa. They played at Boy's house because Hockey's parents were too involved, too likely to check in on them. And thought the role-playing was a bridge to the occult. Boy's grandparents were never around to spoil anything.

Boy heard a yowl.

Outside, the Lundbergs had gotten hold of a farm dog. Four-wheeler engines purred and buzzed, purred and buzzed, as they tied him with a rope to the back. They rode him through the field, and laughed.

Boy covered his ears. He pulled Sarah's tape from his bag, put it on the stereo. He cradled his head in the headphones, pushed them tight with both hands, and listened to the music. He only heard the music. The Smiths.

Sarah went running through the St. Vinnie's, a fur coat in her arms. Spots were worn through, but it was long. Sarah and Boy play fought over it, but it was definitely Boy's. Fit him snug, and had a perfect length for the arms. Boy modeled in the mirror, and Sarah laughed, petting his back.

Boy pulled the coat tight at his chest, and pointed a toe. He cocked his head left. He cocked his head right. He swiveled his head left. He swiveled his head right.

They went for ice cream, the fur in a brown grocery bag in the back seat of her car. She dared him to wear it in to the Dairy Freeze, but he wouldn't.

"Caleb is coming up from Milwaukee this weekend," Sarah said. Caleb was Sarah's boyfriend. He went to an Arts-focused high school.

"A school without a football team," said Boy. "A kind of heaven."

"He's staying with his Dad. You busy?"

"D&D on Saturday," Boy said.

"Geek," she said.

"Bitch," he said.

"Church, then," she said. Sarah had met Caleb at a Lutheran Church camp, and wrote him a letter every Tuesday. Boy couldn't go with her to camp because he worked summers, handing out buckets to families who picked their own strawberries.

The next night was no noise from the Lundbergs. Their kids—what, seven? Eight?—all stayed in.

Boy stayed up later, drawing and sort of reading Douglas Adams. He also half thought about the game, and the new story he'd come up with. A kingmaker, a Bishop assassinated, political struggle for the throne. No mere dungeon crawl, bashing goblins and picking locks. Boy had spent time working on the back-story, the character. Lots to gain and lots to lose.

But he figured on steering Hockey—the only one left in Boy's D&D group—throughout the twists and turns. He always did. Didn't appreciate the time and work Boy put in. Hockey just wanted to kill things and get drunk.

Boy turned on his stereo to listen to Sarah's tape again. He covered himself in the fur and stroked the sleeve, and listened to "Bela Lugosi's Dead."

The bats have left the bell tower. The victims have been bled. Red velvet lines the black box. Bela Lugosi's dead.

His fingers were buried in the fur. One found a rip in the pocket and his erect penis. His stroked it, eyes closed. He pinched the skin at the base hard just to feel it sting.

Undead, undead, the song said.

And Saturday, he waited in the window. They had planned 9. But Hockey never showed on time ever for anything. That's what Boy knew. Boy waited in the window and he wondered when Hockey'd show. He'd walk away from the window, but leave enough of himself there to always also be back. His belly would knot when he was waiting. For this. For other things: for Christmas morning, for the last bell of a school day. His belly knotted. And he waited in the window for his friend.

Hockey came and drank soda and played. And spiked the soda with the liquor from Boy's dad's cabinet, mixed suicides.

Boy saved the vodka for himself, lingered on it to keep sharp, poured just a finger at a time. Hockey gorged on all of it, and pummeled his way through the game. His new character swung an axe at anything that moved and wasn't prone to meditating on consequences. Boy tried hard to rein him in.

Boy's grandparent left them to themselves all day. As they would do. Boy was smart. And got along well on his own. And he loved them. And they loved him. He didn't mind the space between he and them. No father he had ever known. Mother in Minneapolis, high on this or that.

He and Hockey smoked the cigars on the porch. Boy made fun of the way he played. Hockey made fun of Boy's plotline for the campaign. They passed a bag of chips between them.

Boy was sad to see him go. He said, "See you Monday."

Sunday, Boy went to church, though his grandparents had stopped attending. Sarah's dad took them. Her Milwaukee boyfriend, Caleb, was in the car.

Caleb had a head of quills for hair and an ear with ten earrings. He and Sarah sat close at church, and sang from the same hymnal. He hugged Boy when the minister told everyone to greet their neighbor and bid them peace, and when he held Boy, he held strong. Boy returned the hug, and hated Sarah for her luck.

But only for a moment.

After church, Sarah's dad gave her some money, and they walked to a diner called Tommy's to have coffee and an early lunch. They drank the coffee and talked, wasting the counter stools for a couple of hours.

Boy wanted to live in Milwaukee, and attend the arts high school. He had a stud in his ear, but now he wanted more. Hoops of silver. Thin chains of silver that attached to beads. A stretched hole with a thick, black plastic disc.

Caleb held Sarah's hand, and they kissed and shared a cigarette. Sarah had a golden, chin-length bob, and was wearing a dozen bracelets on her left hand. Caleb ordered more coffee and wore black polish on his fingers. Sarah took a drag and blew smoke into Caleb's open mouth. Boy drew them on a napkin. "That's pretty good," said Caleb.

Sarah went to the bathroom. Caleb asked a question. Boy answered, saying out loud something he'd never said out loud.

"Can't be easy, living in a place like this. Sarah says you're a role-playing geek, too. I used to do that. You'd like Milwaukee High School of the Arts," he said. "You'd like it there. You should move."

"My family couldn't afford the tuition," Boy said. "Never in a million years. I'm here until I'm 18."

"Not long now, then," Caleb said. "I know someone you'd think was pretty cute. And, bonus, he's a geek, too." Caleb laughed, and Boy wiped spilled coffee off the table.

"Don't fuck with the dungeon master, Caleb," Boy said. Boy chewed a fingernail and smiled.

Sarah came back and asked if it was time to get out of there. She was talking to Caleb. Boy had disappeared. Boy had become the napkin holder. Sarah wanted to walk back to Caleb's dad's house.

"My grandpa's picking me up soon," said Boy. "I'll see you at school tomorrow." They left Tommy's and Boy watched them walk off. He sat on a bench and waited for his grandpa, who was late and grumpy when he arrived as if he had only just woken up.

"You can tell me stuff," Hockey said.

"We're friends," Hockey said.

"I'm just saying," Hockey said.

Hockey sang along to a song on the radio, sometimes adding the word kike and sometimes adding the word nigger to the songs, making himself laugh. When he did, Boy stared. "You only do that to bug me," Boy said. Hockey sang along with Aaron Neville:

"I don't know much. Cause I'm a *nigger*." Boy looked at Hockey and rolled his eyes.

Hockey smiled, and his bottom row of teeth had flakes of tobacco on them. You take the friends you can get.

Boy took a long walk late at night, and found himself under Hockey's window. He scooped up a snowball, but didn't throw it. Instead, he just sat down, his back against a fencepost. Instead, he sat and stared up at the window. Instead, he bumped his head against the fencepost, gently.

Hockey's driveway was protected by a rusting suit of armor, a statue his father had purchased. It was circled by a low, wooden fence. The tops of each post held a pyramid of gathered snow, and the driveway edges were a line of slush, banking the cleared asphalt. The house was newer than the others in the neighborhood, and had more glass, and a long, high roof.

Hockey's room had a little deck where Boy and Hockey would go to smoke when Boy slept over.

Boy hadn't slept over in a long time now that they were seniors.

Last summer, Boy let Hockey invite some friends over to play basketball at Boy's house. He had an old hoop, and a flatter driveway than Hockey. Boy sat the game out.

The game was shirts and skins, and it was hot. Hockey was tan and round—sort of fat, really, jiggling but also strong—and playing skins. Boy sat on the trunk of Hockey's car and smoked. The game was three on three, and Hockey played rough, throwing himself into the other players. No one called fouls. Hockey's friend Jason took an elbow and scraped his knee when he fell. Boy went inside and grabbed a clean towel.

Boy wiped at Jason's knee, and watched the muscle above the kneecap twitch. Jason smirked and leaned back a little, giving Hockey the finger. After a moment, he grabbed the towel and pushed Boy away.

They called him Nurse and laughed. Hockey called him Nurse and laughed. "Oh, Nurse?" They got in Hockey's car after, and drove around, dropping the friends off. Then, Boy and Hockey stole a couple of beers from Hockey's dad, and drove down to the beach.

On the ride in to school Monday, Boy told Hockey he had stopped by his house the night before. "It was, like, three, though, so I didn't want to wake you."

"What did you do?"

"Just had a smoke. I thought about waking you. I thought about it."

"You were there?"

"For, like, an hour or something. Just needed a walk."

Hockey told Boy he thought it was weird that he would do that.

And Boy told Hockey it was weird. And then, they talked about other weird things.

Hockey dropped Boy off at the door nearest his locker, and went to find a parking space.

A Lundberg—the shorter one—cornered Boy and pushed him into his locker.

Hockey came in and saw. And walked over. And laughed.

"Even your friend thinks you're a fag," said the Lundberg.

Boy went hot. And his knees shook.

"Dead. Your fighter's dead, Hockey," he said.

And Hockey hit him hard, breaking his nose. "Queer," he said.

A night near that one, Boy couldn't sleep and went out for a walk. He went out to the field and wore the fur coat. It was cold and his breath came out light gray in the bare light. Boy scanned the field, and held the coat tight.

The Lundberg brothers were somewhere. Boy heard a buzz somewhere distant. They were riding around. They were yelling to each other, but Boy couldn't tell what they were saying. He walked to the jack pines and blended into the trees—and went low down, on his hands and knees.

He pulled the fur closer. He pulled it closer. And it pulled closer. He was on his hands and knees. He was wrapped in fur. His arms felt long, his legs short. He heard a buzzing, getting closer. He heard the Lundbergs, getting closer. He was on his hands and knees, and he began to move. The Lundbergs came closer, and they yelled. Boy darted left, and they followed. Boy darted right, and they followed. They tried to keep up and they whooped. Boy darted. On his hands and knees, he gained distance on them. He hid in the trees, and pulled them along. He panted and darted. The Lundbergs fell back, trees in their way.

He smelled the snow, and the prickly, burning scent of gasoline. His ears cocked this way and that, he listened for the Lundbergs, and tumbled forward to get away. His eyes were dim and the world was gray, but he knew the scent of home, and keeping low between the trees, moved in that direction. He broke out of the trees, to the field—a strawberry field in spring and summer—and bolted across to his yard.

Boy got more distance, and he made it home. He went up to bed at four. The Lundbergs were still out, riding around, hooting to one another.

Boy walked to the window and watched them. They rode around and around, circling the field, kicking up snow. The taller Lundberg stood up on his four-wheeler, bouncing at the knees. The shorter Lundberg rode by him close. They searched, wove in and out of trees.

Boy stepped back from the window and let his eyes unfocus. He sat on his bed and let his eyes go unfocused. He leaned back, and the ground slipped out of his sight. He heard the Lundbergs yell, and saw the leafless tops of the trees, and the sparse clumps of black on the jack pines. He saw the sky, and the stars, and lost the ground completely. And he believed, for a moment, and then for longer, that the ground had disappeared. He lost the ground, and floated high above, safe.

glory

"Go in peace to love and serve the Lord," he says, and we all get up to do so, or to do something else, instead. Depends on who we are.

Wood, Toddler and I grab our boards from the trunk of Wood's car. We ride over to the funeral home parking lot. The building is empty, abandoned. No one yells at us to move along. On the way we push off on parked cars and avoid the bumpier side streets. We find the smooth new pavement. Toddler hits a rock, and skips forward off his board, and almost falls. He gets his legs under him, though. He runs it out. He chases his board to the curb and catches up to us.

At the parking lot, Wood and Toddler grind the concrete parking blocks that line the edges. They leave behind shavings of metal. Their trucks are grinding down. The bolts are grinding down. The slick wooden decks are wearing through. The stickers on the bottom are peeling off. The plastic rails are almost gone and it has been a long, dry summer.

A teacher's strike has given us an extra month off. It's August and we should be in school tomorrow. Instead, we'll probably come back here. The Escanaba schools will be open, so it's just going to be us and the truants.

And the cops, who will stop us and ask what we're doing. We'll say we're from Gladstone. Teacher's strike.

I'm shirtless, ribs and stuck-out hipbones, lying on my board.

"You need to eat, or something," says Wood.

The grip tape on the board scratches my back.

A car rolls by and someone inside shouts: "Skate fags!"

Wood raises his middle finger. He has long fingers. When he flips someone off, he curls the other fingers to his palm, and mashes them down with his thumb. He has a long, long middle finger, and he can raise it high.

Toddler and I cock the index and ring fingers when we flip someone off. The final knuckle of each frames the middle. It makes Wood seem all the more certain of what he is doing.

The car that is rolling by squeals and stops.

We yell back. We raise our middle fingers. We react to insult.

But, we don't fight.

We run down to the beach, cutting through yards. We go where the cars can't. We run until we get to the beach, and then we stop at the beach house. Wood asks us if we saw how big the guys in the car were. "They were big," he says. "Big."

We buy sodas at a 7-11, and Toddler steals a pack of gum. He gives us each a piece, and throws away the rest, tossing it to the ground.

I've got my hands in the pockets of my shorts as we skate away.

Wood tries a pop shove-it, but gets tangled up. His board rolls away as he watches, leaning over, hands on his knees.

acknowledgments

Much appreciation and thanks to Shya Scanlon and Ryan Boudinot for early help and support. And my folks and brother for even earlier help and support. Thanks to the teachers (esp. Angela Fountas, Adria Bernardi, T.M. McNally, Stacey D'Erasmo, Laura Hendrie, Michael Martone, and Victor LaValle), the Wallies (esp. Lili & the boys, and Amy Minton), the print and online editors, the Giants (esp. Blake and Gene and Adam), the Hobart folks (esp. Elizabeth Ellen and Aaron Burch), the writers who came through my bookstore and encouraged me (esp. Amy Fusselman, Amelia Gray, Jonathan Evison, Leni Zumas, and Michael Kimball), the Yoopers (esp. Tom Bissell—Thanks. A lot.—and honorary Yooper Matt Bell), and the booksellers (esp. Stesha Brandon and Brad Craft). Thanks to Jarret Middleton and Aaron Talwar for giving this book a publisher.

Mostly, thanks to Abby, who was with me through it all.

Dark Coast Press

Dark Coast Press publishes works of literary fiction, fiction, poetry, abstract and experimental writing. We publish established and unknown authors. We encourage writers to take risks and encourage readers to follow them into uncharted territory. We would all like to know what is found there. We love crazy books. Old and new ones. Unfathomable ones. Calm and clear ones. Simply put, we publish books we like.

OTHER TITLES FROM DARK COAST PRESS

An Dantomine Eerly • Jarret Middleton

Thirteen Fugues • Jennifer Natalya Fink

Swell • Corwin Ericson

League of Somebodies • Samuel Sattin

Hell Called Ohio • John Hamilton • September 2013

Check us out online at

WWW.DARKCOASTPRESS.COM

CPSIA information can be obtained at www.ICGtesting.com
Printed in the USA
BVOW070302110613

322983BV00002B/135/P